Parties, Predicaments and Undercover Pets

KT-385-245

I bit my lip and studied Kyra out of the corner of my eye. She looked grumpy; disappointed by my lack of enthusiasm. Maybe I should try to be a bit more encouraging. After all, she *did* love animals. Maybe her parents *would* melt, as soon as they saw Mushu's button eyes and mini-whiskers.

"By the way," I asked, fumbling in my blazer pocket for my bus pass, "is Mushu a boy or a girl?"

"Oh ... I don't know. Doesn't really matter, though, does it?"

Hmm. And then again, maybe this whole Kyra-having-a-kitten thing was a very *bad* idea indeed.

I liked Kyra a lot (even when she bugged me). But somehow I worried that there was about as much chance of Ricky Martin becoming our new school janitor – whistling "La Vida Loca" as he disinfected the boys' toilets – as there was of Kyra Davies being a responsible and reliable pet owner...

Find out more about Ally's World and Stella Etc. at
www.karenmccombie.com

PARTIES, PREDICAMENTS AND UNDERCOVER PETS

KAREN McCOMBIE

for "Sweet Charisma" - whoever you are.

This edition produced for the Book People Ltd in 2006,
Hall Wood Avenue, Haydock, St Helens WA11 9UL

First published in the UK by Scholastic Ltd, 2002

Copyright © Karen McCombie, 2002
Cover illustration copyright © Spike Gerrell, 2002

10 digit ISBN 0 439 95151 8
13 digit ISBN 978 0439 95151 7

Printed and bound by Nørhaven Paperback A/S, Denmark

10 9 8 7 6 5 4 3 2 1

Contents

PROLOGUE

Dear Mum,

You know something? I really wish you could see our pets – they're all so cute. Well, maybe not the stick insects: it's pretty hard to find *them* cute. Unless you're Tor, of course.*

And today was Cute Central round our house, mainly because Grandma decreed that it was going to be Doggy Bath Day. She had a point – Rolf and Winslet *have* been starting to honk a bit lately. (Why is it that cats smell of ... nothing much, but dogs pong of Eau de Old Dog Food and Unwashed Clothes really easily?)

Anyhow, Rolf loved the bath and the fuss, and splashed around biting soap bubbles while me and Tor tried to avoid being drowned by the tidal waves he was making. Then it was Winslet's turn, only it wasn't, because that keen nose of hers had whiffed doggy shampoo and alerted her to the fact that she was about to face the indignity of being soaked. But after a half-hour search by the entire

Love family, she was finally dragged growling from the back of the airing cupboard (Colin gave her away by sniffing at the door) and dumped into the bath, where she stood rigid with resentment while Rowan sculpted her soapy fur up into a mohican.

The cats loved it all, taking it in turns to amble past the bathroom and check out the dogs' humiliation. Not that Rolf minded (or noticed) being humiliated – right now he's lolloping damply outside in the garden, happily sneezing shampooey sneezes. *Winslet* knew the cats were sniggering at her though, and got her own back by shaking herself dry all over Colin and Co, giving them an unexpected shower.

Anyhow, the reason I'm telling you cute stuff about the cute animals is basically to soften you up … before I tell you about the hassles I got myself into recently. Correction: the hassles one of my so-called best mates got me into. And that mate just happens to be Kyra Davies.

Now, why aren't you surprised…?

OK, I'll leave you to read this: I've just heard Tor yelling that Rolf's eaten a bee (again), so I guess we'll be going for a little stroll round to the vet's (again)…

Love you lots,

Ally

(your Love Child No. 3)

* I haven't got anything against stick insects, by the way – it's just that I prefer things that you can cuddle. Cuddle a stick insect, and it snaps. Try and explain *that* to the nice RSPCA man who comes to check on complaints about animal cruelty...

Chapter 1

KYRA AND THE ART OF BOREDOM

The time: 2.30 p.m., Saturday.

The place: my kitchen table. Not that you could *see* my kitchen table for the mound of plastic carrier bags piled on top of it (all from clothes shops, and practically all Kyra's).

"Aren't you a bit scared of it?" Sandie blinked dubiously at the thing Kyra was holding up against her chest.

"Huh?" Kyra wrinkled her freckly brown nose in reply. "It's a *top*, Sandie! How can anyone be scared of a *top*?"

I knew what Sandie meant, of course. (That's what best friends are for; to understand – in some spooky, unspoken, psychic way – exactly what you're wittering on about.)

"It's 'cause it's only got the one shoulder," I started to explain, pointing at the blue-, lilac- and pink-striped top.

"What about it?" Kyra frowned, holding it away from her now and studying it for signs of one-shouldered scariness.

Up until this point, Grandma had been busy-beeing over by the worktops, wiping away grubby finger- and pawprints while "tsk"ing quietly at the mess that made up most of our kitchen. But now that Kyra was holding up her newest, just-bought-an-hour-ago purchase, I spotted Grandma sneaking a peek and doing a bit of frowning herself. I knew the pattern and the colours would be *way* too loud for Grandma's grey-and-navy-tinged taste, but the lopsided shape of it was definitely scoring nil points in her eyes, I could tell.

"What I mean – what *Sandie* means is that that sort of thing is OK if you wear it and just stand *still*," I continued with my explanation to Kyra. "But once you start dancing at the party, aren't you afraid it might … I dunno, *slither* down on one side and you'll pop out?"

"Oh, *right*…" nodded Kyra, catching my drift. "*I* see what you mean. Don't want to end up like Rachel, do I?"

We'd all heard (and shuddered over) the horror story of what happened to Jen's sister just a couple of weeks ago. Rachel had been at a friend's sixteenth birthday party, and thought she must be doing some *majorly* groovy dance moves the way everyone – especially the lads – was staring at her.

It was only when she felt a slight breeziness in the bosom department that she realized her boob tube had become a *waist* tube.

Oh, the *shame*…

"Will you be wearing a bra with that, Kyra?" Grandma butted in.

Good *grief*, Grandma. Just get personal with my mates, why don't you?

"Uh, I don't know," Kyra replied, throwing me a quick glance and trying not to giggle at the bluntness of my gran's question. I know Kyra really likes my gran and everything, but there *is* something weird about being thirteen and having a discussion about bras with a sixty-year-old woman. I don't know why that is exactly … it just *is*.

"Well, dear, it's just that if you wear a strapless bra with it," Grandma carried on matter-of-factly, "you could fix your top to your bra with a tiny safety pin, right out of sight under your arm. See?"

"Oh, yeah!" Kyra nodded earnestly, while nudging me with her foot under the table. Sandie, meanwhile, was staring straight down at the table, her face like a furnace.

Honestly, what was Grandma going to embarrass me with next? A friendly, girlie chat about periods? She was only here this Saturday because of the party next door and, much as I loved her, I kind of wished she'd tootle off and help Michael and Harry butter their burger buns or something instead of mortifying me and my friends and making poor Sandie turn *puce*.

"Oops! Looks like Michael and Harry are firing up the barbecue already!" Grandma suddenly noted, striding purposefully out of the back door. "Better go and take in the last of the washing before it ends up smelling of charcoal and burnt sausages!"

"Wish *I* was going to a barbecue today instead of going out for a *boring* tea with my *boring* mum and dad," Kyra sighed, as the three of us gazed off out into the garden at the flapping washing and billowing grey smoke.

That "boring" tea, by the way, was *only* at Planet Hollywood in the West End, where Kyra's parents where treating her before they took her to the movies. Tough life, huh? But Kyra Davies, if you hadn't noticed already, *loves* a good moan. I think she uses the word "bored" more than the word "and" in her vocabulary. I mean, yeah, so I'd been invited to Michael and Harry's do this afternoon, but it was just a little party for neighbours, which *I* thought would be sort of fun, but Kyra would probably find it *monumentally* "boring".

Still, that's Kyra all over. Her, me and Sandie

had just spent two hours scouring the shops in Wood Green for something to wear for our school's end-of-term party this Thursday, and she couldn't work up any enthusiasm for that either, even once she'd spotted the one-shouldered scary top. And even the trousers and shoes she bought to go with it hadn't exactly raised her excitement levels. "It's only going to be the same old faces we see every day at school anyway," she'd yawned, as we'd trudged around TopShop. Well, maybe; but me and Sandie were well up for it. OK, so if you're some glamour-spangled celeb or some super-cool supermodel, *sure* you might get blasé about the vast amount of party invites that flop through your letterbox and clutter your hallway, but when you're me and are lucky to get one invite a *decade*, any party's a good party.

In fact, I was looking forward to the whole of this last week of school before we broke up for the holidays. For a start, Monday was "Write On!" day, a great idea – authors and magazine writers coming to do talks – with a truly terrible name. (Somebody sack whichever teacher came up with that cornball idea.) Then, on Tuesday, it was the school's annual prize-giving day. (Didn't suppose I'd be coming back weighted down with trophies from that, unless they did one for "Most Useless At Maths".) Then, on

Wednesday, our year had opted to do a sponsored Fun Run round Alexandra Palace, which looked like being a hoot. Well, trundling through the park having a laugh with my mates was a *definite* improvement on the usual Sports Day and all the pain that *that* involves. (I think I got a silver for "Tripping Over The Most Hurdles" last year.) Thursday, of course, was the party (yes!!), and Friday was a mere half-day till the freedom of summer holidays beckoned (bliss...).

All in all, a brilliant, hardly-doing-any-*real*-lessons-at-all, fun week.

"God, this next week at school's going to be such a bore!" Kyra groaned, slumping her elbows on the table and propping up her chin with her hands.

I met Sandie's eyes over the top of Kyra's fizz of bushy ponytail. She rolled her big baby blues and gave me a look that translated as, "Urgh! She's off again!"

"How come you always manage to see the dull side to everything, Kyra?" I grinned at her.

"It's a talent I have," she replied sarcastically. "Anyway, it's all right for *you*, Ally Love."

"*How* is it all right for me?" I asked, totally confused. Call me dense ("You're dense!"), but didn't we have practically identical lives? Didn't we go to the same school, take the same lessons, hang out with the same bunch of mates?"

"You've got all this!" she announced, sitting up straight and flinging her arms out wide.

I glanced round the kitchen, at the teetering stack of dishes drying in the rack; at the practically antique (i.e. rusty) fridge with its "*Absolutely* DO NOT TOUCH *my Onken yoghurt, on pain of* DEATH!! *love Linn*" Post-it note stuck on the door; at the overflowing bin (contents of which included one empty Onken yoghurt carton, courtesy of Rowan); at the 50%-extra free sack of hamster bedding and tins of cat food that I'd forgotten to tidy away after my and Tor's outing to the pet shop that morning; at the gently dying herbs in pots on the window sill that we all kept forgetting to water; at a cat that wasn't Colin contentedly shedding hairs on the comfy pile of clean clothes in the laundry basket.

"What am I supposed to be looking at?" I asked blankly.

"This brilliant family! This brilliant house!" Kyra enthused.

"Are you kidding?" I squeaked. I mean, I knew my family were brilliant, but the house? I loved it, with all it's mad stuff and stupid colour schemes, but it wasn't exactly a show-home, not like Kyra's designer-flash house in one of the poshest streets in Crouch End. "This place is crumbling! Just this week Dad's been panicking over a new crack in the back wall that's as wide as the Thames!"

"*And* the flush handle fell off the toilet when I went five minutes ago," Sandie chipped in.

"Exactly!" I said, slapping the table for emphasis and making one of the carrier bags squeak in surprise.

"And you've got all these gorgeous things…" Kyra bent over and cooed at the squeaking River Island bag, which turned out to be Colin, sticking his whiskery ginger nose out at her from under all the shopping.

"Yeah, the cats *are* gorgeous," I admitted, reaching out and rummaging beneath the layers of plastic for Colin's ear to scratch.

"*And* the dogs, *and* the rabbits, *and* the rest!" Kyra pointed out. "Your house is always fun to come round to – there's always something going on. My place is permanently neat and perfect and boring. *And* my parents are totally boring – they've never let me have a pet!"

"Hmm…" I muttered, remembering that not so long ago, Kyra was moaning to me and Sandie about how messy her family life was, what with her mum's drinking problems. If *I* was Kyra, now that all that hassle seemed to be in the past, I didn't think I'd be complaining about how peaceful things had got at home. But then *I'm* me, and *Kyra* is mental.

"You two have *no* idea," Kyra sighed theatrically, slumping down on to the table and staring nose-to-nose into Colin's green eyes, "how completely BORING my life is…"

"Now what's all this?" asked Grandma, bustling back into the kitchen with an armful of tea towels and Tor's Spiderman PJs. "Only boring people find life boring, Kyra, dear!"

Ooh, I remembered getting this talk when I was about four. It had probably only been raining for about half a minute, but when you're little that can feel like three weeks, and I'd begun whingeing on about being fed-up. Grandma started coming out with that exact same thing about only boring people finding life boring and before I knew it, she had me, Ro and Linn making *kilometres* of paper-chains to keep us occupied. Mum joined in, helping us to hang them up, so that by the time Dad got in (dripping) from work, our whole house had been transformed into the scene of a fiesta. All that was missing was a Mexican mariachi band and a few buckets of Doritos.

"But Mrs Miller," Kyra started to whine. "You don't understand what it's like!"

Uh-oh – Kyra'd better put a lid on that whining malarkey, or Grandma would have the coloured paper, scissors and glue out like a shot.

"Kyra," said Grandma firmly, fixing a schoolmarmish stare at my friend. "What I understand is that you are a very intelligent girl –"

Debatable, Grandma, debatable.

"– and I have every faith in you using some of that intelligence to work out *how* you can stop yourself from being bored and what you can do to be more positive and change things for the better!"

Kyra narrowed her eyes, as if my gran had just rattled off a sentence in Swahili and Kyra was now trying to work out whether she'd asked her the time or for directions to the nearest water buffalo or something.

"You mean," Kyra said slowly, "that I should just get on and *do* stuff, and it'll make me feel less bored?"

"Well, yes; more or less," Grandma nodded. "It's called being proactive."

"Oh," mumbled Kyra, mulling that over.

"Now, can all of you girls be a bit proactive right now and get this table cleared, please?" Grandma ordered us cheerfully, as she started folding the tea towels.

Immediately, I began scooping up bags – and

Colin – from the table, but then I paused, spotting something worrying.

That certain, scheming *glint* in Kyra's eyes. Trust me, that's never, *ever* a good sign…

Chapter 2

SHRIEKING, SCUFFLING AND SAUSAGES

"Don't move!"

I froze, a nacho only a few tantalizing centimetres from my mouth. Rowan – who'd been just about to cross her arms – was now rigid in a looky-likey karate pose. Not that you see many karate experts dressed in dyed red, oversized dungarees with matching red gerberas* pinned into their ponytails.

(*Gerberas are big, coloured daisy things, not to be confused with gerbils, which are not red and do not make good hair ornaments.)

"Why can't we move?" me and Rowan frowned in unison. Of course we'd still done what Tor had told us to. Our brother doesn't say stuff for nothing. (Mostly, our brother doesn't say much at all.)

"Shh!" he shushed us.

What was this? Musical statues? All around us in Michael and Harry's garden, people were busy chatting and laughing while small, neighbourhood kids ran in and out of the forest of legs. Officially, as oldest small kid on the block, Tor was in charge of shepherding the teenies away from the dangers of the barbecue (*and* the prongy barbecue forks which two little boys had tried to poke each other's eyes out with earlier), but he'd obviously broken off from his duties to alert me and Ro to something Very Important. And Possibly Alarming, from the earnest expression on his face.

"You were just about to squash it!" Tor whispered, pointing to the minuscule ladybird currently taking the weight off her rounded wings on Rowan's upper arm. Sure enough, if Ro *had* folded her arms as she'd been just about to, pretty Miss Ladybird would have been no more than a small, squished red dot on my sister's lightly tanned skin.

"Aww! Isn't it beautiful!" cooed Rowan, raising her elbow up, all the better to study the spotty bug. "'*Ladybird, ladybird, fly away home...*' How does the rest of that nursery rhyme go?"

"'*Ladybird, ladybird, fly away home... Before Rowan Love splats you out of existence*'?" I suggested.

"Meany!" Rowan grinned at me, just as Tor leant forward and gently, expertly blew on the bug and sent it fluttering off to safety.

"Still, if you *had* splatted it, Ro, you couldn't have picked a better party to do it at," I shrugged cheerfully. "I mean, Michael could have fixed it up. Done mini-micro-surgery on its little legs or something."

Tor stared at me, trying to work out whether I was joking, or whether his buddy the vet was as all-powerful and all-healing as he suspected.

"He might have had trouble giving it mouth-to-mouth resuscitation, though!" Rowan grinned back at me.

Tor rolled his big, brown eyes at us and shuffled away, now that he realized we were fooling around at an innocent insect's expense.

"Hey, what are you two talking about?" said a friendly voice, as a tray piled high with mustardy-smelling hot-dog buns was wafted under our noses.

The voice belonged to Harry, Michael the vet's boyfriend.

You know, pathetic as it sounds, it still makes me feel a bit ... well ... *funny* saying that. About Harry being Michael's boyfriend, I mean. It's not that I feel weird about the two of *them* – y'know – being *gay* and everything; it's just that the word "boyfriend" sounds kind of silly, when you're talking about two grown-up men. It's the same as Grandma having a boyfriend, I guess. (She and Stanley were over by the greenhouse at that precise moment, nibbling at some sausage rolls and pointing at roses.) Maybe it's just that "boyfriend" and "girlfriend" should only be used by young people, and they (whoever "they" are) need to come up with a new word for anyone over thirty. Actually, Linn once told me that some people who are together but not married call each other "partners", but I think that sucks. It's like it's got something to do with businesses and lawyers or something, and nothing at all to do with soft and fluffy love and stuff.

"So? Come on! I've been watching you two gabbing away for ages. Spill all!" Harry smiled, as I crammed my nacho into my mouth and helped myself to a hot dog.

You'd like Harry. He's really sweet – kind of shy when you first get to know him (whereas Michael's big and boomy), but friendly as anything once you get chatting. He does lighting for big theatre shows and once, when he came round to pick up his bike that Dad had repaired for him, he told us lots of gossip about how bitchy and grumpy actors can be behind the scenes. (Who'd guess that a main star would put itching powder in the costume of another actor who was getting *way* too much applause? I thought stunts like that only happened in the *Beano*...)

Anyhow, Harry's really interesting, so I was sure he didn't want to know that the less-than-riveting subjects me and Rowan had covered in the last few minutes were (in reverse order)...

a) The near-splat of a small insect.

b) Why hot dogs look disgustingly slippery and floppy, but taste great.

c) The fact that Rowan wasn't going to her year's end-of-term party, 'cause she doesn't really have any proper mates at school. (Sad but true.)

d) Friends: how they can drive you crazy, even though you like them. It's like ice cream – eat too much and you feel as if someone's ramming pick-axes into the nerve-endings of your teeth, but you still want more. (Interesting metaphor – Rowan's; annoying friend we were discussing – me, and no prizes for guessing who *that* was.)

e) How irritating it was that Linn could look so effortlessly gorgeous, even when she was just slobbing about (well, as near to slobbing about as neat-freak Linn ever gets) in a pair of jeans and a T-shirt.

f) Who the trendy-ish couple were that Dad and Linn had been talking to for the last ten minutes.

g) The tragic state of Mrs Tiernan's bottom: our neighbour from across the road obviously thought she looked *well* foxy in her flashy silk sarong, but the material was so thin you could see her cellulite through it from the other side of the garden. (Blee!)

"We were talking about this Fun Run Ally's doing at school." Rowan answered Harry's question without missing a beat, or bringing up the rest of the embarrassingly banal rubbish we'd been wittering on about. "I was telling her she should ask all the neighbours to sponsor her while we're here, at your party."

Ooh, nice one, Ro, I thought approvingly.

I'd totally forgotten that that was one of our conversation topics: *her* bullying me into asking neighbours to sign up, *me* wimping out and whispering that I was too shy to ask.

"Good idea!" beamed Harry. "Brought your form with you?"

"Yep," I smiled shyly, dragging one crumpled printed sheet and a biro out of my back pocket.

"Right – hold this, Rowan!" ordered Harry, passing the tray of hot dogs to my sister. "I'll be the first of the neighbours to sponsor you!"

"Speaking of neighbours," mused Rowan, while deciding which hot dog to help herself to, "who's that over there? The couple speaking to Linnhe and our dad, I mean?"

"Hmm?" Harry squinted up from the form he was scrawling on. "Oh, that's Simon and Aisha ...

something-or-other. They just moved into a flat at the bottom of the road last week. Michael invited them when he saw them unloading their furniture van."

"They look ... nice," Rowan murmured thoughtfully.

By nice, I knew that Rowan meant she quite liked their clothes. (Oh, yes, she can be that shallow.) They weren't dressed remotely in typical Rowan kitsch, but they did have on hipper-than-hip, straight-out-of-a-style-mag type stuff.

Personally, I thought the bloke's calf-length combats and scruffy hair made him look like an overgrown schoolboy, and his yellow sunglasses were downright silly. (What's the point in wearing shades that are the same colour as the sun?)

"Yeah?" said Harry, with a hint of a grin. "Couldn't say if they're nice, really. Only spoke to them long enough to find out that he's an actor, she does ... something that I can't remember, and their kids need locking up."

"Huh? Why do they need locking up?" I asked, at the precise moment that Rowan came out with "Huh? He's an actor?" (Shows the different ways our minds work. My quizzy, worrisome mind wanted to know what the problem was, while Rowan's lit up inside with floodlights at the mention of something as glamorous as acting, *dahling*.)

"Seen two little dark-haired boys running around?" Harry asked, handing me my sponsor form and taking the tray back from Rowan.

"The ones with the lethal-looking barbecue forks?" I asked.

"The very ones!" Harry nodded solemnly. "I caught them trying to poke Tabitha awake with the pointy end of a kebab stick."

"Oh, that's not very nice," I winced, thinking about Michael and Harry's genteel, elderly, Queen Mum of a Persian cat.

"You can say that again, Ally," Harry replied with a wry smile.

"So what's he been in?" Rowan twittered, to Harry's total confusion.

"She's talking about the actor bloke," I mumbled apologetically, translating Rowan's babble.

"Well, if you're that interested, let's go over and I'll introduce you," Harry shrugged, and began leading the way across the lawn.

Rowan didn't spot it, but Harry winked at me. Something told me he liked this actor bloke about as much as his cat-prodding kids (i.e. not a lot...).

"Ah, here are my other two girls!" Dad beamed at us as we approached. "Rowan, Ally ... this is Mr and Mrs Finch!"

"Catch you later!" said Linn, excusing herself with a smile, and a secret wink, just for me, as she passed. What was it with all this winking?

"Oh, please! Call us Simon and Aisha!" the bloke boomed, like he was on a stage or something. I took a step back so he wouldn't damage my eardrums.

His wife beamed insipidly by his side.

"Rowan here was very keen to meet you, Simon," said Harry. "She's very into drama."

True, no one else can make an entrance like Rowan, not in the sort of clothes *she* wears.

"Really?" Simon nodded, rubbing his chin and striking the sort of pose you see male models do in catalogues.

"Oh, yes!" Rowan nodded back. "I'd *love* to be an actor ... or even something behind the scenes – like a set designer or something!"

(Fair enough, Rowan is artistic. The only problem would be that knowing her, every set she designed would have to have fairy lights and glitter balls – which might not work too well for historical dramas.)

"Acting's hard graft, let me tell you!" Simon stated sagely, while pushing the bridge of his yellow glasses further up his nose. "But the rewards, ah, the rewards ... they're *very* hard to put into words. But after a great performance, you feel it *here* –"

He pounded himself in the chest.

"– in the *heart*."

Oh, *please*. Did he think he was going for an Oscar with that little speech?

Simon's wife gazed adoringly at him, as did a starstruck Rowan. Dad and Harry were smiling broadly, but I noticed them exchange fleeting glances, their eyes twinkling like they were in serious danger of starting to snigger.

"Wow..." muttered Rowan. "So, what would I have seen you in?"

"Well," shrugged Simon, "you probably won't have seen my theatre work."

"He's just finished a run doing a Pinter at the Queen's Head Theatre Pub!" Aisha nodded enthusiastically.

"Oh!" Rowan gasped, still sounding impressed, even though I knew she didn't have a clue what Aisha was on about. I didn't either, but then I knew enough to be less than impressed by this big-headed bluster. A theatre *pub*? That wasn't exactly some huge West End stage, was it?

"Um, so have you starred in any TV stuff?" I heard myself asking.

As soon as I said that, I was aware of Harry

shuffling by my side, and I *swear* my dad put his hand over his mouth to hide a grin.

"As I was telling your father earlier, I've done *EastEnders* and *The Bill*," Simon smirked.

"Really?" Rowan practically squealed. "What did you play in them?"

"Well, small but crucial roles," Simon rubbed his chin.

"He played someone who bought bananas off a stall in the market in *EastEnders*," Aisha jumped in, bursting with pride, "*and* he was a dead body in an episode of *The Bill*!"

"I had to lie still for *hours*!" boomed Simon. "It took *tremendous* concentration!"

Dad was *losing* it. That was no coughing fit he was having – he was trying to cover up a case of the giggles!

"And you did that advert for fabric conditioner last month, don't forget!" trilled Aisha, oblivious to Dad's badly covered up, mild hysterics.

Good grief. Tom Hanks and George Clooney would be shivering in their Hollywood shoes at the competition from this bloke.

"Wow..." Rowan sighed, still starstruck, for no apparent reason. (That sister of mine is *such* an airhead sometimes...)

"So what about you, Ally," Simon stunned me

by turning his attention my way. "Are you as keen on acting as your sister?"

"No, but she's really good at writing," Dad replied for me. "She always gets great marks for her essays!"

Mr Actor's eyes glazed over. If we weren't going to be talking about him or acting, then he wasn't terribly interested – that was pretty easy to spot.

"Oh, yes! Of course!" Harry nodded encouragingly, pausing to let some passing neighbours help themselves to the the hot dogs he was carrying. "Tor told us that you two wrote a song together recently!"

I couldn't help beaming for a second, even though "Not Enough..." was hardly likely to be heard on MTV any time soon. It was hardly likely to be played in a grotty student *bar* anywhere soon: according to Rowan, her mate Chazza's band were on the verge of splitting up after a big argument about their image. Chazza and a couple of others liked their slightly grungey look, while the other half wanted to go psycho goth and do the whole mental, Marilyn Manson, black-lipstick and ripped-Lycra look. (If you've never seen that, don't bother checking it out – it's pretty gruesome.) Somehow, I couldn't see Chazza bare-chested, in a pair of shiny leggings and platform boots.

Personally, I'm sure his faded long-sleeved black T-shirt, cruddy jeans and battered Converse baseball boots would have to be surgically removed before washing…

"Well, the song was kind of fun to do," I shrugged shyly. "But I do other types of writing as well … stories and stuff. And I quite like writing poems too."

"Hey!" Harry chuckled. "That's just reminded me of something I used to do at school!"

I waited expectantly, while his memory drifted back a decade or three. Meanwhile, Mr and Mrs Actor were starting to look distinctly bored. (What a cheek – when Harry worked for a proper theatre and everything!)

"I had this little black notebook I scribbled in *all* the time!" Harry continued, scratching his dark hair ruminatively with the hand that wasn't holding the hot-dog tray. "On every page I wrote something different … sometimes a lyric of a song I really liked … or maybe a really clever saying someone had come up with. Jokes too! And there was some of my own stuff … poems and thoughts and things. God, I wish I still had that!"

That sounded kind of cool. At least it sounded more fun than a diary, when you have to write in it every day – even on the days when nothing much happens except you get up, do nothing much and go back to bed fourteen hours later.

"So it's like a *journal*?" I asked tentatively, liking the worthy, grown-up sound of that word.

"Yes…" Harry nodded thoughtfully. "It's like an *inspiration* journal."

Ooh, I liked the sound of that even *better*. It was something Grandma would probably be suitably impressed by – there was nothing boring about an "inspiration" journal. I wanted to start one straight away. I wanted to nip home and rummage around my desk and in my boxes and see if I had any small notebooks that would fit the bill, otherwise I'd have to go to the stationery shop up on Crouch End Broadway and get—

My trail of non-boring, inspirational thoughts was interrupted by a flurry of shrieking, scuffling and sausages. It took a few seconds – and some filling in from Tor later – to work out what had gone on, and then the horrible, embarrassing truth sank in…

Lured by the tantalizing waft of sausages, our determined dog Winslet had launched an SAS-style assault on the party, bypassing the wall in between the two gardens and burrowing under the fence at the far end, entering someone else's garden altogether, then burrowing under the fence at the end of Michael and Harry's.

She'd slinked into the garden on her tummy (not hard to do when your legs are about five centimetres long) and, even without the aid of a balaclava, she could have successfully completed her mission – i.e. getting back to ours with a mouth full of uncooked sausages – if two small, dark-haired boys hadn't spotted her and tried (and failed) to harpoon her with a barbecue fork.

And that's the bit *I* saw.

"Oi!" I yelled, leaping towards Mr and Mrs Actor's brats, in an effort to save Winslet from a serious pricking. "Leave her alone!"

At the same time as I lunged, Mrs Actor started shrieking, "Lucas! Felix! Get away from the nasty dog!"

I'm *sorry*? OK, so Winslet was growling at the harpoon kids, but who exactly had the pointy sharp barbecue forks in their hands?

Before I got over to them, everything changed, happening in slow motion. First, Lucas or Felix or whichever little monster it was, took a kick at Winslet. Thankfully, Winslet has the skills and grace of a hairy (and canine) Michael Owen out on the pitch, darting and dodging any attack. She bounced smartly to the right (string of sausages still in her mouth), so that the kicking kid stumbled forward, straight into the path of Tor, which wasn't a good idea. Even at *my* distance I could see that Tor was incensed with rage at the idea of anyone trying to a) hurt an animal, and b) hurt *his* animal. In fact he was *so* incensed that he did something totally out of character.

"Ooooowwwww!"

He kicked the kid.

Hard.

Right on the shin.

The kid started yelping, his brother started yelping, their mother started screeching and everything went slightly bonkers. Including Rolf barking frantically from the other side of the garden wall.

"Tor! Are you all right?" I heard Dad's voice (not angry, just concerned) right behind me.

"Er, I'll take Winslet home…" I mumbled apologetically to a bemused-looking Michael (who'd been manning the barbecue) as I scooped my thief of a dog under one arm and tried (unsuccessfully) to prise the long trail of linked sausages out of her mouth.

"OK, OK!" I whispered to my quietly growling bundle of fur and bad temper, hurrying through the house towards the front door, before Mr and Mrs Actor demanded that Michael – as a vet – should have Winslet put *down* or something.

Oh, well … that was one party ruined. Just as

well I had another one to look forward to this week. And let's face it, nothing as embarrassing could happen there, could it?

Um...

Chapter 3

HUP! TWO, THREE ... *URGH...*

"You're ... *huh, huh* ... really lucky ... *huh, huh...*" panted Billy.

"And you're really unfit," I told him, as we jogged along one of the zillions of paths that zigzag across the hilly park surrounding Alexandra Palace.

I wasn't sure if he heard me though, what with all three dogs barking (and in the case of Precious, *yapping*) as they ran alongside us.

"Can we ... *huh, huh* ... sit down for a second?" Billy glanced at me pitifully.

"Sure! If you really need to..." I laughed, not letting on how grateful I was to see that upcoming bench.

The dogs didn't seem to have noticed that we'd put the brakes on, and carried on lolloping and barking their way along the path, into the leafy distance.

Ah, well ... they'd be back soon enough. Especially once they realized that neither me, Billy or the handful of doggy treats I had stuffed in my back pocket were anywhere in sight.

"Some help *you've* been with my training," I teased Billy, hoping I didn't sound as breathless as I felt. "I thought you were meant to be fit? I thought you played football all the time?"

Usually, me, Billy and the mutts meet up on Sunday mornings for strolling and yakking, but this particular day Billy had promised me that we'd be pounding the hills, getting me geared up for Wednesday's Fun Run. So far we'd been running for about ... ooh, two minutes, and even though I was feeling marginally less half-dead than Billy, I suddenly wasn't holding out much hope of earning my sponsorship dosh off the neighbours. (Who were luckily all very sweet the day before when I went back to the barbecue after double-locking our arch-criminal dog in the kitchen – except for the snotty actor *et famille*, who'd scarpered in a huff).

"Football's ... *huh, huh* ... different," Billy panted some more, putting his baseball-capped head between his knees to stop himself from passing out or something.

"Sorry, I forgot – football's that game where everyone gets pushed around on comfy armchairs eating crisps. Right?" I baited him.

"Mmmnumphhh," he mumbled incoherently.

"Anyway," I carried on, staring out over the

green slopes at the variously shaped dogs and their owners dotted here, there and every grassy where. "What were you saying about me being lucky?"

"Your school," Billy replied, sitting upright and starting to sound a little less like he was in imminent need of an oxygen tank. "At least they're giving you a few good skives this week. Not like *my* stupid school. *And* they're giving you a party."

Poor Billy – I'm sure going to an all-boys school isn't good for his health. I'm sure the absence of girls in any form for the major part of the day is the reason he gets planet-sized crushes on *any* member of the opposite sex at the drop of a hat. Girls in bands, girls on ad posters in bus shelters, girls working in local shops (at least Anita went out with him for all of five minutes), girls in films, girls in computer games, girls who are pictured on the *Readers' True Experiences* pages of my magazines… Billy can come over like a lovesick puppy at two seconds' exposure to a pretty face.

Me … OK, so I'm guilty of random crushes too (apart from my one true love Alfie, even though he's blindingly unaware of it), but at least I think that daily close contact with the nose-picking, teacher-baiting, semi-obnoxious ways of the lads at my school makes me a *teeny* bit more selective and realistic about my crushees.

"I can't believe your school isn't even having a *party*," I shook my head.

(Out of the corner of my eye, I could see a solitary Winslet – always the smartest, if grumpiest, dog in the pack hurtling back along the path in our direction. Of course, when I say "in our direction" I mean "in the direction of the doggy treats".)

"What's the point of having a party with 1,206 other boys?" shrugged Billy. "What am I going to do? Ask Hassan or Richie if they fancy a dance?"

"It would be all right – as long as you didn't ask them for a *slow* dance!" I grinned wickedly at him, as Winslet skidded to a halt on the path beside us and laid her head appealingly on my feet.

(Oh, yeah? Like I can't spot doggy blackmail when I see it?)

"So what are the teachers going to do with you this week?" I asked Billy. "Just make you work as normal?"

"Oh, no, no, *no*." Billy shook his head wryly. "They've got *lots* of exciting things lined up."

"Like?" I asked, spotting the distant galumphing bound of Rolf coming back along the path, followed by a small white yapping frenzy of poodle.

"Oh, let me see..." Billy said thoughtfully, rubbing at his chin. "I think the highlight would have to be … the quiz our chemistry teacher has lined up for us!"

"Yeah? So what kind of quiz is it?" I said, as Rolf came baying towards me through sheer happiness at finding his long-lost (one minute and counting) owner.

"It's a *chemistry* quiz, Ally," Billy replied in a wearisome way.

"And if you win…?" I asked, while pushing the loving tongue of Rolf away from my face – which *had* been washed today already, thank you.

"I think the winner gets a bunsen burner or a test tube or something," Billy muttered.

"That sucks," I agreed, as Precious came yappity-yapping up to us.

"Ally, when you're thirteen, life has a tendency to throw many sucky things at you," Billy sighed, just as an excitable Precious – fresh from his exhilarating run across the park – starting clambering on Billy's leg and doing *very* dodgy-looking aerobic doggy exercises.

"That's brilliant!" I gasped, simultaneously grabbing a notepad (a sweet purple one that came free with a copy of *Girltalk* magazine aeons ago), a pen and some doggy treats out of my back pocket.

"What are you doing?" asked Billy, watching me

chuck a handful of crunchy nibbles way over on the grass.

"First, I'm stopping Precious from doing whatever he's doing," I explained, flicking to a fresh page. "And *now* I'm going to write down what you just said."

"What? About the bunsen burners?" Billy frowned.

"No – that stuff about being thirteen and many sucky things coming your way," I explained, as I clicked my pen into action.

"Um ... why?" Billy quizzed me, staring at the notebook – sorry, *journal* – that was already crammed with my favourite jokes, song lyrics and lines out of poems we'd done in English. (Oh, yes – I'd been up late last night after the barbecue, getting my new project up and running.)

"It's something I've started doing," I answered. "Writing down my thoughts, or funny or interesting stuff I hear."

"Is that something they've made you do at school?"

"No. It's something I *want* to do."

Billy frowned at me as if I'd just announced I was going to be writing a thesis on the molecular structure of *mud* during the summer holidays, just for fun.

"Don't worry," I smiled at Billy, yanking his baseball cap down over his crinkled-up, confused nose. "Just keep saying funny stuff."

I couldn't see much of Billy's face (since I'd pulled his hat over it) – all that was visible was his lovely, dumb grin.

Oh, yes, I mused to myself. *This journal is never going to leave my side. I'll scribble down everything brilliant I come across, and in years to come—*

"Brrrrrrpppppp!"

Suddenly, Billy let out a huge, rumbly, I've-had-beans-and-sausage-for-breakfast burp, just at the same time as I noticed Rolf squaring up for a poo.

Good grief. It's hard to get inspired when everyone (and every dog) around you is a complete and total heathen...

Chapter 4

FEARGAL THE FEARLESS

Squeak! Squeakity-squeet!

"...and then I worked for *Smash Hits* magazine before—"

Squeet!

"Oi! You lot at the back! Quit it *now*!" Mr Samuels (our English teacher) roared, as the slightly startled-looking woman standing beside him at the front of the class blinked at the loudness of his interruption. It had obviously been a long, *long* time since she'd been in a classroom, and it seemed like the constant misbehaving/teacher roaring/momentarily behaving/misbehaving again/teacher roaring cycle was a bit of a shock to her system.

"But, Sir! There's something wrong with these chairs!" grinned Feargal O'Leary, as his cronies snickered beside him.

(The cronies: Mikey D, Mikey F, Ishmail and Baz. Their function in life: to snicker at everything Feargal does and says.)

"Shut it, Feargal!" Mr Samuels growled. "I've

had enough out of you this morning. Miss Gray here has taken the time to come and talk to us today, and so the least we can do is listen. Right?"

"But, Sir!"

"Shut it, Feargal! And for the last time, put your hood *down*!"

It was Monday, it was about ten to lunch, and I'd just sat through a morning of talks from a variety of writers, in the company of a very weird mixture of people from my year (i.e. Feargal and Co, amongst others). I'm not sure why our normal classes were broken up and muddled together for these "Write On" sessions, but I'd found myself with only Kyra and Jen for close company. Who knows which writers Sandie, Chloe, Salma and Kellie were with, I only hoped they were more interesting than the lot we'd been subjected to. I mean, a writer from the *Telegraph* newspaper, who was boasting about his prize-winning feature on the gross national product of Guatemala? *Please!* Had he mistaken us for a bunch of fifty-year-old businessmen? Had he mistaken us for people who cared?

And then there was the bloke who made up crosswords for national magazines. Fascinating. But not as fascinating as the woman who worked for *Concrete Today* magazine. Or was it *Tarmac*

Monthly? I can't remember, since I lost my will to live somewhere during her talk. No wonder Feargal O'Leary and his mates were acting up. Mind you, they *always* act up. They are, officially, the bad lads in our year – although no one seems very sure what bad things they get up to, other than cheeking the teachers and looking tough.

Feargal O'Leary looks the toughest of all the lads, even though they all wear identical hooded sweatshirts under their blazers (hoods worn up whenever possible), with matching slouches and scowls (when they're not snickering wickedly). But I've got a theory about Feargal and why he acts the way he does; I just reckon that it must be hard to be the leader of a tough boy gang when you're name is Feargal O'Leary – and you're black. Being lumbered with the name of an old, Guinness-drinking Irish bloke must be a pain in the neck when you're a cool young black guy. What were his parents thinking of? OK, so your parents can't help what your second name is (that's just a fact of long-lost family history), but "Feargal" for a first name? Even the Irish lads at our school think that's funny. It almost made me feel sorry for him...

"Anyway, after I left *Smash Hits*," Miss Gray continued, once Mr Samuels gave her a nod, "I found time to start writing this book, which I based on my teenage diaries. Does anyone here keep a diary?"

Oops – before I'd had time to think of the implications (i.e. looking like a total nerdy swot), my hand shot up in the air.

"Pffffftttttt!"

Of course, I couldn't be sure exactly where that jeering snicker came from, but I had a fairly good idea. So did Kyra, swinging round in her seat beside me and shooting daggers towards the rear of the class and Feargal's lot.

"Yes?" the woman smiled encouragingly at me.

"Go on, Al!" Jen whispered at me, nudging my ankle with her foot (ouch).

"I ... um ... don't keep a diary, exactly," I gulped, trying hard to sound confident, but sure I was failing miserably. "It's more of a ... a thing that I carry around with me to write stuff down in. Like a ... a..."

God, this was going to sound so pretentious.

"Like a what?" Miss Gray prompted me.

"– a journal. Well, a journal thing. Kind of."

"Pffffffttttt!"

Urgh.

"Really?" Mr Samuels nodded at me. "And what do you keep in this journal, Ally?"

"Um ... I just scribble things in it, things people

say, or what I'm thinking..."

"*Pfffffftttt!*"

"...and I write down bits out of my favourite songs..."

"*Pfffffffffffffffftttttt!*"

"...and bits of poems," I blushed, wishing I'd never stuck my stupid hand anywhere except across my mouth. I'd only started the stupid thing yesterday – it was hardly a life-long passion. What did I have to go and talk about it in front of everyone for?

"*Pfffffffftttttttttttttttttttttttttt!*"

"You lot! Enough!" Mr Samuels barked in Feargal's direction.

"Your own poems, er, Ally, isn't it?" Miss Gray carried on regardless (though I wish she hadn't bothered).

"Some..." I shrugged miserably. "Some by real poets too."

"Have you got it with you now?" Miss Gray smiled at me.

"Yes..." I replied dubiously, curling my fingers around the soft cover of the small notebook in my blazer pocket.

Oh, good grief – she wasn't going to ask me to read something from it, was she? *Please* let Martians beam me out of this classroom, *please* let Martians beam me out of this classroom...

"Well," smiled Miss Gray, who I was really beginning to dislike, "I'm sure we'd all love to hear—"

The bell! The glorious, ear-splitting *Braannggg!!!* was music to my ears! Me and my stupid journal were spared!

"I'm sure everyone would like to thank Miss Gray for a very interesting and informative talk!" yelled Mr Samuels over the screech of chairs as everyone bolted for the door and lunch.

"Thank you, Miss Gray," I mumbled, along with forty other mumbles from all around me.

"*Thank* you, Miss Gray! *Thank* you, Miss Gray!" someone squealed sarcastically in my ear.

I turned round to find Feargal (hood in regulation "up" position once again) pushing past me through the surge of escapees, staring at me as if I was a particularly horrible nodule of fungus.

"Look at *me*, Miss Gray – *I've* written a journal!" he squealed again, pulling a face while the lads surrounding him snickered away at their Lordship's excellent jest (not).

"Ignore him," Kyra ordered me, as I felt myself jostled out of the doorway and into the hall. "He only wears his hood up so he can catch the few brain cells he's got when they trickle out of his ears!"

Good old Kyra. She said that last bit really

loudly, specially so Feargal and Co could hear. Feargal O'Leary might be fearless, but so is Kyra Davies, and it's times like that when I remember why being her friend is a good thing.

"What losers!" Jen hissed, narrowing her beady little eyes at the retreating, cackling bunch of be-hooded boys. "Anyway, see you two after lunch?"

"Yeah – if we can stand the excitement!" Kyra yawned, as we waved Jen off to the school canteen.

"Well," I muttered, heading towards the main exit with Kyra, and idly thinking about the mounds of peanut-butter sandwiches I was going to comfort-eat my way through at home, "that was horrible. What's Feargal's problem? What have I ever done to him?"

"Zero. You were just *there*, and that's a good enough excuse for drongos like him and his brain-dead mates," Kyra shrugged. "Anyhow, forget them – I've got a surprise to show you!"

"Where? When?" I frowned, instantly recognizing that worrying glint in Kyra's eyes.

"Now! And I'm not telling you where – just come with me!" she grinned mischievously.

"Come on, Kyra! You've got to give me a clue!" I pestered her, as we burst out of the door and into the scorching sunlight.

"OK ... it's got something to do with what your gran said on Saturday."

"What – you're going to get a strapless bra?" I blinked at her.

"No," she sighed wearily. "I've decided to stop moaning about things never happening, and *make* things happen. Oh, quick! There's the bus! We've got to catch it!"

And so we sprinted across the road (good practice for the Fun Run, I supposed), and began our magical, mystery tour of Crouch End...

Chapter 5

RUMBLY TUMMIES AND PURRING BLAZERS...

There is nothing very magical about Hornsey Road, and the only mysterious thing about it is how it can look so *scuzzy*. Practically the whole grubby length of it could do with being squirted by a twenty-metre-high bottle of Cif and scrubbed (with a very, *very* large brush) till the grime comes off.

At least Kyra had made us get off the bus at the slightly *less* scuzzy end of the road (i.e. the one with fewer boarded-up shops and dodgy, dusty old men's pubs with windows that look like they last had a wash around the same time as man invented the wheel).

"What are we doing?" I asked, which seemed a reasonable question, since I was glancing around and couldn't immediately figure out why Kyra might be taking me to a carpet shop/butcher's/sub-post office – and that was more-or-less all there was round here. My stomach (unimpressed so far by Kyra's magical mystery tour) was starting to rumble impatiently, and I was beginning to pine for that mountain of peanut-butter sandwiches I'd been fantasizing about earlier.

"*You*," Kyra smirked, pushing me round a corner into a side street and down into a sitting position on a low brick wall, "are going to wait *here* for me, and *I'm* going to go and get the surprise! No peeking at where I'm going! Promise?"

"Promise," I shrugged.

And with that she was gone. And even though I had a funny, fluttery, faintly *dubious* feeling in my stomach about this whole surprise malarkey, I did as I was told and didn't peek. Probably because I didn't want to ruin the pleasure of being presented with the carpet remnant/packet of sausages/book of stamps that Kyra was bound to come back with...

"Ta na!" she grinned, popping up by my side five minutes later.

At first, I couldn't see what she was "ta-na!"ing about. It wasn't as if she was holding anything – except herself. In fact, why *did* she have her arms wrapped across her chest?

And then her blazer mewed.

Uh-oh...

"Isn't it beautiful?" Kyra beamed, as I got to my feet to investigate the tiny, suede-brown face that was peeking out from between Kyra's lapels.

"It's a kitten!" I blurted out in shock.

"Hey, quick! Get the girl on *Who Wants to be a Millionaire*!" Kyra giggled.

"But where's it come from?" I asked, baffled. Was the butcher shop doing a sideline in live kittens? Or maybe the carpet shop had a deal on – buy a rug and get a free cat...

"You know Claire Easton?" Kyra asked me.

"Uh-huh." I wondered what Claire in our year had to do with anything (anything small and furry).

"Well, her cousin lives in a flat above the grocer's shop."

"So?" I shrugged, feeling like we were getting nowhere fast.

"*So*, Claire's cousin's cat had kittens, and she said I could have one," Kyra informed me.

"Whoa!" I held my hands up to stop her. "When did you arrange all this with Claire? I didn't even know you knew her well or anything!"

"I don't," Kyra matter-of-factly answered my question, while she stroked a miniature paw with her finger. "I overheard her talking about the kittens with her mates on Friday, but didn't think any more about it. Then after your gran said what she said on Saturday, I just thought, wow! So as soon as I left your house, I decided to go and see Claire and ask her about the kittens, which was pretty easy to do 'cause I remembered that she lives right across from school, and—"

"What do you mean about what my gran said?" I frowned, watching Kyra snuggle her upturned light-brown nose on the kitten's wriggling light-brown head.

"Hold on!" Kyra told me. "I'm trying to tell you what happened! Anyway, Claire was in, and she said she'd take me to her cousin's if I liked. So we got the bus down here and – oh, Ally – all the kittens were *so* beautiful. They're all part-Siamese!"

"Get on with it," I ordered her, crossing my arms.

"Well, they were all spoken for, except for this little one. Only I couldn't take it away till today, because they and their mum were getting checked by the vet this morning. And I *had* to pick it up today, 'cause Claire's cousin's moving to Brighton tomorrow."

I narrowed my eyes at Kyra (while struggling to resist the temptation to cuddle the kitten – I didn't want to make Kyra think I approved of what she'd done).

"Like I said before – what's my gran got to do with this?" I asked her. "And, anyway, I thought your parents didn't *want* pets!"

"They don't," Kyra shrugged. "But *I've* always

wanted a pet, so I decided to take your gran's advice about making things happen. And as far as my parents go, well, I've decided to hide this *ickle* baby in my room for a while, and then break the news to Mum and Dad when the time is right."

"Huh?" I mumbled, wondering how my grandma had managed to get the blame for this. 'Cause I *could* be wrong, but I think it's safe to say that when she gave Kyra that talk about being "pro-active", she hadn't meant for Kyra to go against her parents' wishes and smuggle an undercover pet into her room. I think Grandma just meant for her to stop whingeing a bit.

"Listen ... you can't carry it like that," I said, suddenly worried for the kitten's welfare and for Kyra's sanity.

"Why not?" Kyra flounced huffily, now that she'd noticed I didn't seem to think that getting the kitten was the most excellent idea in the world. Even though it *was* absolutely and totally adorable.

"It's not safe! It could wriggle out of your arms and get squished under a lorry!" I ticked her off, feeling myself come over all über-sensible and Grandma-ish.

"But I thought it would be more fun to *cuddle* the kitten..." she muttered petulantly.

"Not when you're walking along a busy road, Kyra," I told her over my shoulder, as I hurried across the pavement and picked up an empty, cleanish-looking cardboard box from beside the grocer shop's overflowing bin.

"Sulky" was the only way to describe Kyra's expression. Still, however reluctant she was, she gently plopped the bemused brown kitten into the box I was now holding open in front of her.

As I fastened it closed, my eyes skimmed on to my watch.

"Omigod! Look at the time!" I yelped. "What are you going to do with the cat? It's going to be hard enough to make it back for class – you won't be able to take it home first!"

"I'm not *going* to school this afternoon," Kyra announced, carrying the box tenderly in her arms as we crossed the teeming road to the bus stop that would take us back up to Crouch End.

"What?" I squealed (nearly as loudly as the brakes on the car that I hadn't noticed nearly running us down). "What am I supposed to say to the teachers?"

"Don't care. Say I felt sick and went home," Kyra shrugged in that irritatingly shruggy way she has. "My mum's out today, so I'm going to cut classes and get Mushu settled in."

"Mushu? Like the dragon in the Disney film?" I asked, thinking that the skinny, mewling fluffball in the box didn't have much in common with a smart-talking, Chinese dragon.

"Yep, from *Mulan*. That's what I've decided to call it," Kyra nodded, watching as our bus nudged its way through the traffic towards us.

I bit my lip and studied Kyra out of the corner of my eye. She looked grumpy; disappointed by my lack of enthusiasm. Maybe I should try to be a bit more encouraging. After all, she *did* love animals – you could see that from the way she turned from Miss Smart 'n' Cynical to Miss Mushypants as soon as she set eyes on any of our menagerie. Maybe her parents *would* melt, as soon as they saw Mushu's button eyes and mini-whiskers. Maybe having something to love and look after would be really good for Kyra.

"By the way," I asked, fumbling in my blazer pocket for my bus pass, "is Mushu a boy or a girl?"

"Oh ... I don't know. Claire's cousin did tell me, but I've forgotten. Doesn't really matter, though, does it?"

Hmm. And then again, maybe this whole Kyra-having-a-kitten thing was a very *bad* idea indeed.

I liked Kyra a lot (even when she bugged me). But somehow I worried that there was about as much chance of Ricky Martin becoming our new school janitor – whistling "La Vida Loca" as he disinfected the boys' toilets – as there was of Kyra Davies being a responsible and reliable pet owner...

Chapter 6

SOGGY CABBAGE AND STARING TORTURE...

"Ally *LOOOOVVVVEEEEE*!" a voice reverberated along the corridor towards me.

Oh, no.

"My office, *now*, please!"

This wasn't fair. I'd wanted to spend my lunchtime stuffing my face with peanut-butter sandwiches and hauling Rowan away from the telly long enough to moan to her about my freak show of a morning, thanks to Feargal O'Leary and his meat-head mates. Instead, I'd been dragged (OK, bussed) to the other side of Crouch End, been forced to witness Kyra buying herself a real live fashion accessory, and done a chest-busting, heart-exploding, Fun-Run-winning sprint from the W7 bus stop into school *just* after the bell had gone.

And then I go and get spotted by none other than the she-devil who just happens to be our Year Head.

Poo.

"Yes, Mrs Fisher," I mumbled breathlessly, as I

was diverted away from the class I was supposed to be in and made to follow the she-devil to the labyrinth of doom (i.e. her office).

"Sit!" she ordered, pointing me down like a disobedient labrador pup.

I sat, feeling my cheeks flush pink – first from running and rushing and now, from pure humiliation. I don't suppose anyone gets a *kick* out of getting into trouble (actually, people like Feargal and Co suddenly spring to mind), but me – I seriously stress out about it. It's not that I'm a total goody-goody (I mean, I'll happily giggle about the terrible two-sizes-too-small clothes our science teacher Miss Kyriacou wriggles herself into in the name of non-fashion), but I try really hard never, *ever* to get into any bother, mainly 'cause I couldn't bear the sad look of hurt disappointment on my dad's face if I ever messed up.

But thanks to Kyra Davies, here I was, about to get shouted at. Which – along with everything else that had happened so far today – was making this so-called fun week at school start off pretty poorly, if you ask me.

Mrs Fisher stared at me silently for a few seconds, which is her preferred form of torture. I think she enjoys seeing you squirm and sweat for a bit before she finally tears you to ribbons.

"Alexandra –"

Oh dear. She was using my proper name – I was *so* in for it.

"– *just* because this is the last week of term, doesn't mean you can get away with *murder*."

Wow ... I must be losing my mind. There I was, thinking that my only crime was to zoom through the main school doors twenty seconds late, when all the time I was *actually* a serial killer. My, my – how careless of me to forget...

"Eep," I mumbled under my breath in a useless kind of reply, wringing my hands together and trying not to meet the gaze of the mad old coot.

"If you get into bad habits like lateness now, and are *not* punished for them, you will *only* carry them into the next term," she barked at me, in that tone of voice that told me I wasn't expected to stick up for myself or answer back.

"Eep," I squeaked in a practically inaudible voice.

"And speaking of late – where is Kyra Davies? Didn't I see you two running off to the bus stop together at the start of the lunch hour?"

I felt like sneaking a look around her room to see where the false wall was; the one that would open up Austin Powers-style to reveal a bank of telly screens, linked to every CCTV camera in the area.

It was the only way she could be so all-seeing. Good grief: did she have a camera in the loos too? Had she spied on me and Chloe doing our excellent (i.e. excellently cruel) impressions of her stomping prune-faced around the corridors?

Arghhhhh...

"Well?" she demanded, as I tried to push the vision of Chloe strutting past the sinks, wrinkling her nose as if every pupil at Palace Gates School smelled of old, cooked cabbage.

"Well..." I began, raising my eyes to look at Mrs Fisher and seeing that Chloe was spot-on; from Mrs Fisher's expression, it was obvious that I did indeed smell to her of soggy cabbage. "Well ... Kyra and me ... we were just going up to the Broadway ... for ... er, *something*. But then Kyra started to feel ... ill."

I was winging it, making up lies on the spot and feeling not only Mrs Fisher's withering glance, but that telltale muscle quiver in my face that always starts the minute I come out with porky-pies.

"Ill?" Mrs Fisher snarled.

"Um, yes," I shrugged, hoping inspiration would strike soon and help me make up something that would satisfy the evil Mrs Fisher and get me out of her dungeon before she got the thumb-screws out. "She ... she got a stomach ache, and had to go home. And … and that's why I'm a bit late. I was making sure she got home all right!"

Liar, liar, pants on fire. It's a wonder Mrs Fisher couldn't see wisps of smoke wafting from my knicker department from her side of the desk.

"I *see*," Mrs Fisher muttered ominously. "Was anyone home with her? Her mother or father?"

"Um, no," I shrugged.

"Right, then," she sighed, getting up so fast she practically *crackled*, and walking over to a filing cabinet. "Better find a work number for one of her parents – let them know Kyra is ill."

See? *This* is why I hate lies so much; it's like amoebas or something. You start with one, and they keep multiplying, till you've got tonnes of the slippery things slithering around, out of control.

"No! I mean, it's OK … her mum … was only out shopping," I blabbered, probably hideously unconvincingly. "Kyra was expecting her back any time!"

Mrs Fisher froze with the drawer marked *A–F* partly opened, and fixed me with one of those long, *looonnngggg* hard stares of hers.

And then she stared at me some more, just for that *extra* tweak of torture.

"Very well. You're excused."

THUNKKKKK!!

The reverberating metallic clang of the filing-cabinet drawer was like a very dramatic, very LOUD full stop to what she was saying. I bit my lip and tried to figure out whether that meant I could leave or not – it was hard to tell from the way Mrs Fisher had now returned to her seat and stopped looking at me. (Be grateful for small mercies.)

"What are you waiting for?" she suddenly glared up at me, still superglued to my chair with fear. "GO!"

Two seconds later, I found myself walking along the corridor (bad choice of words – *wobbling* along the corridor would be better, since adrenalin had made my legs turn to rubberized jelly), aching to get to my class and slink into my seat next to the comforting silence of Sandie. She'd be worried about me by now ... wondering what could have—

It was a long corridor; a *very* long corridor. It was made up, as corridors tend to be, of mostly wall and a smattering of doors. As classes had already started, most of these doors were firmly and safely shut, so that *if*, say, someone with abnormally wobbly legs who was hurrying too much (i.e. me) was to trip and fall, the chances of anyone spotting this ridiculous event would be, oooh, very small indeed.

But that person would have to be an ordinary person – not terminally unlucky Ally Love.

'Cause there I was, tripping over thin air and skidding flat-faced on to the red lino floor, in full view of the one, open classroom door in this vast stretch of empty corridor. Honestly, *my* luck. If I'd been on the *Titanic*, they'd have managed to wave off every single woman and child to the safety of the lifeboats, all while I'd nipped to the loo. I'd have been left on deck, with just the band and all the blokes for company, and I'd *still* probably have got them all laughing through adversity 'cause of having my skirt tucked in my knickers or something...

"*Pffffffffffffffftttt!*"

You wouldn't have thought I could get any lower than spreadeagled on the floor, but all of a sudden – at the sound of that "*Pfffffttttttt!*" I felt my heart sink with a weary thud.

"Oi! *Nice* knickers! *Not!*" yelled a voice that *had* to belong to Feargal O'Leary. Only it was *kind* of hard to hear him properly, what with the catcalls, whistling and yelping coming from what could only be his meat-head mates.

I stood up, hauling my skirt down to its rightful place, while I tried frantically to remember what knickers I'd actually been wearing...

"Oi, Blue Bum! Not talking?!" Feargal yelled, as I scurried away, in a haze of blushing and sweating.

Ah, so I was wearing my denim-coloured knickers. Well, mystery solved.

Oh, the *shame*...

God, I wish I'd yelled back that crack that Kyra had made earlier – the one about Feargal having to wear his hood up to catch stray brain cells leaking out of his ears. At least that might have made me feel better. But my pathetic, useless brain can only come up with smart stuff like that about three days after the event.

Still, I decided. *I can always write that comment down in my journal.*

OK, so it was way too late to say it to Feargal O'Leary's face, but at least it might make me feel a *tiny* bit better to have it scribbled down somewhere.

I stuck my hand in my pocket, and pulled out ... a snotty paper tissue. And nothing else.

Where was my journal?!

I spun around, to see if it had shot out of my blazer when I tripped, but no – the corridor was an empty, flat sea of shiny, red lino, with absolutely nothing on it except for the odd scuff of black shoe rubber.

Uh-oh.

All my thoughts, rambles and – maybe most embarrassingly – my favourite slushy song lyrics were in there. Who was looking at them (and into my stupid, rambly head) right this second...?

Chapter 7

PETCARE, LESSON 1 – KEEPING YOUR PET ALIVE

"I god a code."

That was the phone message I'd got from Sandie at eight o'clock this morning, when I'd been wiping a dollop of marmalade off my school tie (at the same time as trying to stop Rolf *licking* it off – who needs Essence of Dog Tongue wafting up your nose all day?).

Sandie's *always* getting colds. She must have the weakest immune system in medical history, even though her mum is practically fanatical about her vitamin intake and would make her wear a thermal *bra* if anyone had bothered to invent one.

"You *are* going to phone the school, aren't you? You don't want me to tell them for you, do you?" I'd enquired warily. OK, so Sandie's "code" was genuine, but I really didn't want the responsibility of that whole please-miss-my-friend-is-sick routine again today, specially since it had given me one very big guilt headache yesterday. (Thank you, Kyra.)

"I can't *believe* Fish-Face was actually going to

call my parents at work!" Kyra ruminated, staring off into the distance and shaking her head.

I didn't say anything in reply, mainly because we were in Maths, and – funnily enough – Mr Horace doesn't really like us talking about anything except maths in his classes.

"I mean, she really has got a cheek, hasn't she?" Kyra spun her head round and asked me, in her normal, not-exactly-quiet voice.

I suddenly wished two things:

1) That Sandie hadn't god a code, which meant Kyra wouldn't have stolen her vacant space and parked herself next to me today.

2) That Kyra would go to whispering lessons, where she could learn to talk at a level somewhere *below* a bellow, so that she didn't risk us both getting detention.

I picked up a pencil. (Don't worry – I wasn't going to stab her with it, although the thought was tempting.)

Kyra – although Mrs Fisher comes pretty high on my list of People I Like Least in the Universe, and I'd rather do DIY dentistry on myself than take her side for any reason, I DO think skiving off to go home and play with your new kitten is the thing that's REALLY cheeky here...

OK, I didn't write that exactly. I *wanted* to, but

I had to keep my scribblings short and sweet, since Kyra has the attention span of a minnow.

(That last bit was quite funny; I might have stuck that in my journal – if I still had it. If it wasn't lying in a side street off the Hornsey Road or on the top deck of a bus or wherever else I'd lost it yesterday lunchtime.)

What did your M+D say about Furball? I scrawled instead, then nudged the otherwise blank page of paper across the desk towards Kyra's eyeline.

Kyra frowned, read, then scrawled something back.

Not told them about Mushu yet. Not good time.

Now it was my turn to frown.

Furball still secret?!

Yep, Kyra scratched out in biro. *But it's OK – played music in room till late so M+D couldn't hear miaowing.*

Somehow, I didn't feel reassured.

Where's it sleeping? I scribbled frantically.

Bottom drawer. Can shove it closed if M or D come into room. Smart, huh?

Good *grief*. Rolf Harris would be pulling out his beard hairs in frustration if he heard any of this.

Won't your M find it today while you're at school? I wrote.

She's out all day – no problem.

Well, *I* could think of a problem or two. For a start, small kittens need loads of attention, not to mention grub. Which made me worry about something else...

What are you feeding Furball?

Kyra took her turn, dashing off a reply.

Smuggled leftover curry to my room last night.

Aaargh! Get miniature stomach pump!

Kyra, kittens can't eat curry!

True – it didn't like chicken, but then it was tandoori. Liked rice, though.

Now, I was *seriously* starting to worry about Mushu's welfare. If Kyra didn't have a bed for it and was feeding it tandoori chicken, what were the chances of her making sure it wasn't going to get dehydrated?

What about water?! I scribbled furiously.

What ABOUT water?! Kyra scribbled back, with a shrug of bewilderment.

Honestly, if you asked me, Kyra Davies couldn't even look after a *picture* of a cat, never mind the real thing. What on earth was going to become of—

Swooooppppppp!

"My, my! Furballs ... kittens ... curry... This is *very* interesting!" said Mr Horace, his eyes skimming over the cat waffle in the notepad he'd magically whisked away from between me and

Kyra. "But I have to say, girls, it doesn't seem to have a *lot* to do with maths, does it?"

"No, Mr Horace," we both mumbled – though I swear Kyra said "Horse-Arse", which is the nickname the oh-so-charming and eloquent boys in our class gave him.

Amazingly, Mr Horace didn't seem to catch that, which was lucky considering we were in enough trouble as it was.

"Let's see ... I think I can come up with some extra homework for you to do tonight, just for fun," Mr Horace smiled sarcastically at the two of us. "How does that sound, girls?"

Rinky blimmin' dinky.

Tor would have been proud of me; I was on a mission of mercy (via Kyra's local corner shop).

"There you go, sweetheart!" I murmured, as Mushu practically headbutted my hand out of the way in its desperation to get to the saucer of tinned kitten food.

"God, what's that smell?" Kyra moaned, wrinkling up her nose and staring around her very neat, very stylish bedroom.

I recognized the pong straight away – it was the not-very-stylish scent of wee, amongst other toiletry unpleasantness.

"Kyra, whatever goes into a cat at one end, *has* to come out the other," I informed her.

"Yeewwww!" squirmed Kyra, glancing anxiously around the room for the grisly evidence.

"What did you expect Mushu to do, Kyra?" I demanded. "Keep its little furry legs crossed? Here's a lesson in cat care for you: cats are living things, they are not – repeat *not* – Furbys."

"I know *that*," muttered Kyra huffily. "I just … forgot about the peeing part."

Sigh…

"Well, that's what this is for," I told her, pulling a small sack of cat litter out of the plastic carrier bag on the floor. "Do you have an old paint tray out in the shed or something?"

Kyra looked confused. She was finding it enough of a shock to the system to realize that she was expected to feed and water this creature; she didn't have a clue what strange purpose I might have for a paint tray.

"It's for the cat litter," I explained wearily. "It's probably the best thing you can use till you get to the pet shop and buy a proper litter tray."

"Oh," Kyra nodded, stroking the head of the ravenous mini-beast. "Yeah, we must have one somewhere."

"Well, let's go and look," I said, leading the way

to the bedroom door and out on to the landing.

"OK," Kyra yawned indifferently, as she stomped down the stairs behind me. For her, practical tasks were boring with a capital B.

"And we'll have to get some kitchen roll and one of those spray-on cleaner things to sort out Mushu's little accidents," I continued, in my best taking-control-of-the-situation voice.

"Oh, Ally, can *you* do that?" Kyra suddenly whined, as we reached the downstairs hallway. "It'll just make me sick!"

I was about to tell her where to go (and it wasn't anywhere nice with palm trees and blue skies like you'd see on the *Holiday* programme), when I thought of something Kyra could do in return. OK, call it blackmail if you like – but I only had the poor little furball's well-being at heart.

"Listen, I'll scoop the poop," I told Kyra, spinning around to face her at the bottom of the stairs, "if *you* promise to tell your parents about Mushu today!"

"I promise!" Kyra gushed, sounding well pleased with the deal. "Only, I'll have to wait till Dad's home from work – I've got a better chance of getting round him than Mum."

"Fine," I shrugged. "But promise me you *will* tell them, and *promise* you'll look after Mushu properly!"

"I promise!" Kyra repeated. "Cross my heart and—"

Suddenly, negotiations were halted – a jangle of keys in the front door put paid to that.

"Oh, hello, girls!" Mrs Davies smiled at us brightly, while dropping her handbag down on to the hall table and shutting the door behind her. "Good to see you again, Ally!"

I was just about to say "Hi!" back, when Kyra distracted her mum by yelling at her.

"What are you doing home? You're not supposed to be home today!"

(Translation: "What are you doing home when I've got an illegal pet hidden in my room and I'm feeling really guilty about it?")

"Calm down, Kyra!" her mum frowned at her. "I only popped back to pick up the car! What are you getting so worked up about?"

" 'Cause I never get any space round here! I can't even have my friend back for lunch without you *hovering* around, hassling me!"

"Kyra! There is no need to speak to me like that!"

Urgh. Getting caught up in the middle of someone else's (stupid) fight was *too* horrible. So I did the only thing I could think of and faked a coughing fit.

"Oh, dear! Are you all right?" Kyra's mum asked.

"Yeah ... *cough, cough* ... I've got ... *cough, cough* ... a cough sweet in my bag up in ... *cough, cough* ... Kyra's room," I spluttered, as I hot-footed it up the stairs and left the battling Davies' to it.

And there was me telling my neighbour Harry only two days ago at the barbecue that I wasn't interested in drama. After *that* performance, I could get a part on telly, *easy*. Maybe as a dead body on *The Bill* or something.

I'd just have to try not to cough, of course...

Chapter 8

BLUE BUM, RED FACE

"…and the prize for *blah, blah, blah* goes to *blah, blah* in Year *blah*…"

The drone of Mr Bashir's voice was quite soothing. That, combined with the fact that it was really warm in the school's main hall, was making me feel pretty drowsy. And maybe the stress of keeping Kyra's secret wasn't helping either – after today's deeply non-relaxing lunchtime round at her place, I could happily have done with a small snooze. And where better than in the middle of the annual prize-giving ceremony, in the middle of the entire school population? (I.e. Mrs Fisher would never spot me if my eyelids started to droop…)

"Do you think your Linn might win something, then?" hissed Salma, nudging me awake. "She's pretty clever, isn't she?"

Unlike me, Salma, Jen and Kellie were looking mildly interested in the awards, while Chloe and Kyra – sitting on the other side of me – were flicking through a copy of *Sugar* magazine.

"Maybe she will," I shrugged at Salma.

It would be kind of exciting to see Linn up there, I mused, rubbing my eyes and smelling a faint hint of Whiskas kitten-sized tuna chunks on my fingers.

She's sickeningly good at lots of subjects, my older sister. *And* she has nice boobs, which happen to be in perfect proportion to the rest of her body (chance would be a fine thing in *my* case). *And* she has a very pretty face (when she stops frowning at me and Rowan). *And* she has the most beautiful, deliriously desirable boy in the whole of North London as her best mate. It's not really fair, is it, for one person to have so much going for her? Oh, except that she's related to the rest of the Love family and that drives her totally *insane*.

Ah, well ... every silver lining has a cloud...

"Maybe Rowan'll win an art prize!" Kellie suggested, leaning across Salma towards me. "That collage thing she made was brilliant!"

"Was" being the operative word. Rowan's class had been set the task of doing self-portraits, in whatever style they wanted, so Ro bypassed the paint and the charcoal and did *her* self-portrait in M&Ms. (Oh, yes – M&Ms, as in small sugar-coated chocolate things.)

It *was* pretty amazing. Close up, it just looked

like a bunch of sweets glued on to an A3 sheet of paper, but if you stood away from it, there was this brilliant, multicoloured image of Ro, with yellow M&M skin, brown M&M plaits, and a red M&M flower tucked behind her ear. Her teacher, Mrs Garcia, was so chuffed with it, she hung it – pride of place – in the corridor outside the art department. *Big* mistake. By the end of the first day, every passing pupil had swiped themselves a sweet, till there was nothing left on the wall but a raggedy-looking A3 sheet of paper.

Rowan was *well* gutted, but I did point out to her that the glue she'd stuck the M&Ms on with was probably highly toxic, and she cheered up a bit after that.

"...and next," Mr Bashir continued to drone, "the prize for *blah blah* goes to *blah blah* for his excellent *blah-de-blah*..."

So maybe Linn and/or Rowan might win a prize (i.e. a handshake from Mr Bashir, a "certificate" run off in the school office, and a book token for 25p or something), but I wasn't about to let the vague possibility of that happening put me off my siesta. I was *sooo* tired, I could feel my head begin to melt into sleep...

Thunk.

Oops, someone had accidentally whacked their

foot into the back of my chair. Ah, well, these things happen.

Thunk.

Thunk.

Thunkity-thunk.

Hmm. Someone was being careless.

"And the prize for the naffest knickers – *heh, heh!* – goes to ... Blue Bum!"

"Pffffttttttttttt!!"

I wasn't sleepy any more – having your chair kicked from behind and being verbally ridiculed within hearing range of several rows of people has an odd way of waking you up.

"Oi," said Kyra, swivelling round in her seat, "shut it, Feargal!"

It was nice of her to stick up for me, since I seemed to have become paralysed with embarrassment, and couldn't have managed to turn around if someone told me Prince William had just walked in to the hall. Nude.

"Ignore him," Jen muttered reassuringly, as my other friends tutted in support.

"Not speaking, Blue Bum?" I heard Feargal snigger.

"Pffffffffffttttttttt!" snorted his faithful cronies.

"Didn't you hear what I said?" growled Kyra, swivelling around again. "You lot should put your hoods down – maybe then you won't be so deaf!"

Out of the corner of my eye, I could see that Kyra was grinning; she was quite enjoying this. When you're the sort of person who's easily bored, I guess any little hassle brightens the day. Me, I could easily do without it.

"Yeah? Well, *you* can't be deaf, Kyra – not with ears *that* size!"

In the merest blip of a second, Kyra had rolled up her magazine and landed a resounding whack on someone's – presumably Feargal's – legs. She turned back round with a triumphant smile, just as a nearby teacher grunted at Feargal and Co to be quiet.

And they were. For about ten, whole, blissful seconds.

"You smile, but it makes me shiver,
You look my way and it makes me shake..."

Speaking of shaking, at the sound of Feargal's mocking voice, that's exactly what I started to do. Those were lyrics from the song I wrote with Rowan, and the only place Feargal could have found them was in...

"Every time you talk to me
I'm sure it's just some mistake—"

"Give me that!" I hissed, spinning round and reaching for my missing journal, just as Feargal slinked back, out of grabbing range, while his buddies practically wet themselves sniggering on either side of him.

"There's no point to loving you,
There's no point in all this pain—"

He was going to feel pain in a minute, when I strangled him by yanking hard on his hood toggles.

"Ally!" said Chloe, tugging at my sleeve.

I thought she was trying to stop me clambering over my seat and committing murder; I thought that's why all my friends were suddenly babbling my name.

"Ally!" Chloe said louder. "It's *you*! Mr Bashir's just called your name out!"

Huh? Was I now going to have to go through the humiliation of being told off through an amplified microphone, for all the school to hear?

"You won a *prize*!" Jen said.

"For essay writing!" Kellie grinned. "Quick! You've got to go up on stage *now*!"

And next thing, five pairs of hands were propelling me to my feet and shuffling me past bumpy knees towards the aisle.

Good grief, they weren't joking. People were clapping (not exactly wildly, but after five billion awards, your enthusiasm and clapping power does tend to wane), and Mr Bashir was smiling at me.

Good grief. OK, I'd said that already, but my head was full of mince, and my legs were on auto-pilot, walking me towards the stairs that led up to the stage and the podium where Mr Bashir was standing.

Good grief. Grandma was going to be so proud of me ... and Dad especially. Wow, wait till I told him I'd actually, genuinely *won* something, even if it *was* just a crummy bit of paper and a book token that was so mean you couldn't buy a *bookmark* with it.

"Yo! Blue Bum! Go, girl!"

"Oof! Oof! Oof! Oof!"

Good grief. How to have a special moment ruined – have a bunch of meat-heads baying at you, like they're on the *Jerry Springer* show. Right now, the whole school must have their eyes trained on my bottom, just to check out what was so blue about it.

Urgh ... with that thought ricocheting around my head, I hadn't a clue how I was going to make it up the five small steps to the stage. But I did – well, *nearly*. Instead of treading on stair number five, my traitorous right foot decided it might be more fun to *trip* on it, sending me sprawling floor-wards for the second time in two days.

The gasp from around the hall was like something out of an old, Saturday afternoon movie about circuses. You know – a sharp intake of shocked breath from the entire audience as some lion-tamer gets his arm chomped, or some trapeze artist triple-somersaults into thin air, not realizing that the guy who's meant to catch him is still on his tea-break.

Then the waves of giggling started, led by loud guffaws that had Feargal and Co's stamp all over them.

But you know something? I didn't really care. Luckily for me, the excruciating shooting pains in my ankle were taking my mind *right* off it...

Chapter 9

THE *OPPOSITE* OF FUN

Have you ever seen bread baking? Trust me, it's the *weirdest* thing.

First, you put a small dollop of soggy, floury *gloop* in the bottom of a metal baking thingy and, lo and behold, the yeast in it (whatever yeast *is* exactly) makes it expand and expand and expand until the dollop of gloop *boings* out of the baking thingy, and spills over the sides.

Amazing.

The thing is, it takes a good, long while and a hot oven to make that whole expanding doodah happen to bread dough. When I tripped over on the stage at school and instantly tore a ligament in my leg, it took precisely 0.5 seconds for my right ankle to go from looking like a normal, bony ankle to a bunch of bread dough spilling out over my shoe. (*Bleeeurghhhhh.*)

Or maybe it was more like the time Billy filled a balloon with water and chucked it out of his mate Hassan's fourth-storey window... (Don't ask – it's just a boy thing.) Maybe *that's* more what my hideously deformed, wildly swollen ankle looked like (a water-filled balloon – not a fourth-storey window), when I finally managed to focus on it as Mr Bashir and the deputy head Ms Naik pulled me up off the laminated wood floor and dragged me to the wings of the stage.

That was three hours ago. Now, I couldn't see the alien being that was my ankle, thanks to it being swaddled in a plastic frame and three tonnes of padding and bandage.

Still, revolting alien ankles were the *least* of my worries.

"Omigod! The whole *school* must have seen my knickers!"

"Oh, I'm sure they didn't," Stanley murmured amiably, as he patted my hand.

You know something else weird? Apart from my inflatable, alien ankle? Right then, Stanley's white, hairy eyebrows looked exactly like fuzzy little clouds floating just above each eye. They moved when he was talking … it was very soothing to watch.

"But why … why are that Feargal guy and his mates picking on me all of a sudden?" I continued, to my captive audience of one. "I mean, 'Blue Bum'. How awful a nickname is that? Eh, Stanley? And *how* did he get my journal?"

"Er, I don't know, Ally," Stanley replied, his eyebrows floating around again.

"OK, so Kyra tried to stick up for me with Feargal, but then *she*'s the one who got me into all this trouble with Fish-Face and Mr Horse-Arse, *and* she made me keep quiet in front of her mum about Mushu!"

"I see..." Stanley murmured, frowning and making his hairy clouds bump together.

Actually, I think Stanley had not one single, solitary *clue* what I was going on about, and I don't know *what* was making me babble on so much, but then I think it might have had something to do with the very strong painkillers they'd just given me down at the casualty department of the Whittington Hospital.

"I don't even know which essay I won the prize for!"

"Well, I'm sure that—"

"It's just not fair!" I moaned, tearing my eyes away from Stanley's hairy clouds and glaring at my mummified leg. "This week at school was supposed to be such a skive!"

Ooh, maybe "skive" was a bad choice of word, considering Grandma had just walked into the room with a tray of mugs and biscuits.

"Well," I corrected myself quickly, "not a *skive*

exactly – but it *was* meant to be fun. And so far this week, I've had the complete *opposite* of fun, and it's *still* only Tuesday..."

"Have a biscuit. Take two," said Grandma briskly, brushing my whinges aside with a mound of milk-chocolate Hobnobs. "Stanley, can you pop another cushion under Ally's leg? I think it should be higher."

My gran's seriously lovely. She might not be a "there, there diddums", or "let me kiss it better" type granny, but she's very good in a crisis. Which is why, when the school nurse checked my ankle and said I'd need to go to hospital, it was Grandma I phoned first, and not Dad. (As agreed with Linn and Rowan – who'd swooped round to the nurse's station as soon as they'd seen me go *splat*.)

The way *I* saw it – even though I was busy trying not to pass out with monumental pain at the time – Dad would have panicked, probably run out of the bike shop without locking it up (or worse, locking an unsuspecting customer *in*), cycled to the hospital, then not been able to figure out how to get me, my mummified leg, my crutches and his bike back up to our house afterwards. Grandma, on the other hand, would take precisely no time at all to assess the situation and take control.

Which she did, naturally. Five minutes after the

school secretary had phoned her, Grandma arrived in Stanley's Mondeo, assuring me that she'd called Dad and persuaded him not to flip out as she had everything under control, and next thing I was in the waiting room in the casualty department of our local hospital, with Grandma feeding me mints while her OAP boyfriend Stanley made feeble but sweet jokes.

And now, here I was, recuperating in the quiet, peaceful surroundings of my very own home. *Not*.

"Why did you take me here, Grandma?" I asked, nibbling on a Hobnob and finally noticing properly for the first time that I was in Grandma's flat, and not the madhouse I call home. (Hey, I told you those painkillers were making me woozy...)

"I thought it would be more restful for you here, just for an hour or two," said Grandma, brushing my hair away from my face with her hands.

Which was useful, really, as without realizing I'd started to eat a chunk of it with my Hobnob.

"Your gran thought it would be calmer here, at first," Stanley elaborated. "You know, without the dogs, and the cats and Tor and everyone getting over-excited."

True.

One whiff of an Exciting New Thing in the house (i.e. my mummified leg) and Rolf would have tried to eat it, while Winslet would have growled at my crutches. The cats would have taken turns using my padded, bandaged leg as a scratching post, and Tor would have been gagging to write his name on it with felt pen, even though it wasn't real plaster.

Actually, all that would still happen, but sensibly, Grandma had noticed that my head was on the planet Shocked and Sedated at the moment and was wisely sparing me from my normal home life till I was a bit more like my usual self.

Whatever *that* was...

"How do you think Feargal got my journal, Grandma? Do you think I dropped it and he found it?" I babbled. "Or do you think he might have taken it from my pocket, when he barged past me yesterday after that talk we got from the woman author person?"

"I've no idea, Ally, dear," Grandma said matter-of-factly, as she held a cool hand to my forehead. "Are you feeling all right, or would you like to lie down? You could always doze in my bed if you want..."

Ooh, this was nice. I wasn't so mushy-headed that I wanted to sleep, but the very novelty of being here in Grandma's flat felt like a total luxury, mummified ankle or not.

Grandma's flat is like something out of one of

those DIY shows you see on morning TV (when you're genuinely off school sick, of *course*). It's all cream and beige and sand colours with lots of glass and wipe-clean surfaces. And the few tasteful ornaments dotted about the place are interspersed with classy, silver-framed photos of me and Ro and Linn and Tor and Dad and Mum. Especially Mum, at various ages and stages, which are always fun (and kind of sad) to look at...

"No, I'm all right here," I shrugged in response to Grandma's question, as my eyes settled on a really funny picture on the window sill of me and Billy (my number one, oldest friend) splashing around together in the paddling pool in Priory Park, aged about four. In the corner of the snap, I noticed, was an arm, and the sparkle of tiny mirrored beads sewn into a hippy top. It *had* to be Mum...

"Are you OK?" Stanley and his amazing, floating eyebrows asked me, as he gently laid my mum-mified leg on top of the latest squashy cushion he'd added to the pile on Grandma's beige velvet footstool.

"Yes, thank you," I smiled happily at him. Because however spiky and annoying (and painful) things had been over the last couple of days (or *hours*, in the case of the torn ligament), it felt like a total treat for me to be here in Grandma's calm, serene, elegant flat. Even though she only lives four streets away from us, I hardly ever come round here, just 'cause Grandma is constantly round at our place, cleaning up after us (poor her) and making our tea during the week (lucky us). And on those rare occasions when I *do* come round to her clean and calm cocoon, it's usually in the company of the entire Love clan, or various chunks of it. The idea of me being here on my own, being pampered with the best china mugs, the nicest biscuits, the personal attention, and the cooling touch of Grandma's hand on my forehead, was almost magical.

Magical... I mused, feeling my pain-drenched, pain-killer-befuddled mind drift off.

"Of course, this puts paid to that Fun Run thing you were supposed to be doing around Alexandra Palace tomorrow," Grandma pointed out, yanking me forward by the shoulders and stuffing another cushion behind my back.

Urgh ... she was right.

"And as for that party of yours on Thursday..."

She didn't have to say any more. It was obvious – whatever naff, fun, silly, groovy or brilliant music the DJ chose to play, I'd look like an award-winning *pillock* trying to dance to any of it on my crutches.

Thanks fate! Nice one...

Chapter 10

TRAINERS ... SHORTS ... KITTEN...

"Ally, it's not often you'll hear me say this, but I think you should take the rest of the week off school." (That was my gran.)

"Listen, Ally Pally, I know you don't want to miss out on having a good time with all your friends – since this is the last week of school and everything – but I really think you should at least take tomorrow off." (Dad.)

"Stay off! Oh, go on! Then we can phone each other and moan about what's on daytime TV!" (The still-sniffly Sandie.)

"You did *what*? Ha, ha, ha, ha, ha!" (Billy.)

OK, so the sensible thing to do on Wednesday would have been to take it easy and sit on the sofa with cats and cushions and the remote control. Only I guess I'm not very sensible...

"All right, Ally? Sure you're up to this?" Mrs Fisher frowned at me, like I smelled particularly badly of old cabbage.

See? That's how horrible she is. Anyone else

would take one look at me, wearing this saddo yellow plastic vest thing I'd been given, perched on my crutches in an alleyway that leads out of Alexandra Palace park, and say, "Wow! Even though you're on crutches, you've offered to be a marshal at the Fun Run, helping direct everyone, so you can still do your bit for charity! What an amazingly brave, big-hearted person you are, Ally Love!"

"I'm fine," I shrugged at Mrs Fisher, wishing for once that I had a strict dad who'd *force* me to do as I was told, instead of a really nice one who caved in when I insisted I was fine and wanted to hobble on my crutches to the Fun Run.

(Which took me, by the way, half an hour – just to get from my house to the park. It normally only takes ten minutes when Rolf and Winslet are dragging me there.)

"Well, I'll leave you to it, and go and check on the other marshals then," Mrs Fisher said dismissively, as she strode off. The other geeks in plastic yellow vests, she meant.

You know, I think she delegated me this alleyway deliberately, just to punish me for disrupting the prize-giving ceremony yesterday. (Yeah, like I *enjoyed* the pain and humiliation.) The alleyway must must have been the most boring point in the whole run – the marshals dotted around the park itself would have a great view of all the runners, most of the time. Me, I'd only see them for a split second or three, when they poured out of the park gate and thundered past, before disappearing around the corner into North View Road and going back into the park via another gate. And then I'd have about three years of boredom, till they came round the same way on their second lap. Then another six years before they did their third lap. I should have brought a book to read. Or Billy's Gameboy. Or a candle that I could melt and mould into a wax effigy of Mrs Fisher and stick pins in.

I sighed, wriggled my elbows out of my crutches and sat myself down on someone's garden wall, hoping the flat wasn't owned by some relative of Mrs Fisher's, who'd shoo me off the wall and tell me to stand up straight – injured ankle or *no* injured ankle.

Idly (since I didn't have a book/Gameboy/wax effigy to while away the hours), I stared around the street, which I knew pretty well from my dog-walking drags to the park. All there was to see really was a bunch of red brick houses and flats, but Winslet and Rolf had a lot of dog buddies up and down the road. Somewhere at the bottom lived Rusty (a sweet, dopey King Charles spaniel) and Ben (a really smart, teddy-bear-lookalike shih-tzu). Maybe their owner would pass by with them ... getting licked to death would pass the time a bit. Or there was this really nice, funny old lady called Alice who lived across the road – she was always out at her gate, ready for a yak with anyone passing. She once gave Rolf and Winslet some of her cat's crunchies, so she had life-long, four-legged fans in them. If I hadn't been terrified of Mrs Fisher checking up on me, I might have gone across, knocked at Alice's door and seen if she fancied a chat, or if she could spare a biscuit for a cripple or something.

Actually, speaking of food, I was pretty hungry. I hadn't eaten any breakfast – I'd been too busy badgering Dad into submission and setting off early for my snail-like stump-a-thon to the park. Right across the road from me was a newsagent: maybe I could hop across and get myself a bag of Wotsits before anyone needed me to do any marshalling (i.e. pointing).

I was rustling around in my skirt pocket for change when I heard the rumble and thumping of an approaching stampede of wildebeests. Or maybe it was just everyone in my year. Yikes, they'd come around quicker than I'd expected – the whistle for the start of the race had only gone off five minutes before.

But sure enough, here came the first super-eager sporty types, running as if they were in the Olympics and missing the point that this was supposed to be for fun (and Cancer Research, if I wasn't mistaken).

I was going to stand up and wriggle myself into my crutches, but then I thought, why bother? I wouldn't be able to point if I did that, so I just carried on sitting where I was, quickly hauling my gammy leg out of the way of passing trainers, and stuck my hand out in the direction they all needed to go. And meanwhile felt like a right plonker.

"Hi, Ally!" Jen called out, as she and my other buddies piled out of the gate.

My spirits lifted as soon as I saw Jen, followed by Chloe, Salma and Kellie waving at me like they hadn't seen me for a few decades. Kyra was just behind them, but she wasn't waving. Mainly because she seemed to be carrying a sports bag in her arms.

Huh?

"It's brilliant that you're here, Al!" said Jen, as all the girls drew to a breathless halt beside me.

"Is it?" I wrinkled my nose, wondering what exactly Jen meant by that. Brilliant that I'd come to the race, even though I had a mummified leg? Brilliant that I was sitting on a dusty brick wall in an alleyway? Brilliant that I was here on the planet?

"Yeah – we didn't know where Mrs Fisher had sent you," panted Kellie. "We thought you were maybe on the other side of the park."

Was she kidding? It would have taken me a *fortnight* to hop my way over there.

"Kyra needs you to look after something for her," Chloe grinned, nodding her red head towards Kyra, who was fiddling with the zip of the sports bag.

"What are you carrying that around with you for?" I asked her. "Got a four-course packed lunch with you?"

"*No…*" Kyra replied, just as I was sure I saw the bag move.

"All right, Dumbo? All right, Blue Bum?" I suddenly heard a cackle, followed by several "*Pffffttttttt*"s.

"Get lost!" Chloe snarled at Feargal and his meat-head mates as they slouched slowly by.

The boys were trying really hard to look cool, and (I was pleased to notice) failing miserably. Like everyone else, they were in regulation black sports shorts, but they were all wearing their usual hooded tops – with hoods in "up" position, natch, which is pretty hard to maintain when you're jogging. Every couple of seconds, the hood would slip down on one or other of them, revealing a number one haircut and a pair of dodgy ears, and have to be yanked self-consciously back up into place.

Dumbo – er, sorry, Kyra – stopped glowering in Feargal and Co's direction and turned her attention back to me.

"It's Mushu!" she said, just as a small head popped out of the bag to the delighted *coo*s of all my mates.

"Kyra! What are you doing carrying that around in your bag?" I gasped.

"Mum announced that she was going to be at home this morning, and said she was planning on cleaning my room," Kyra babbled. "So I had to take it with me! And don't frown at me like that, Ally! There's airholes in this bag so it can breathe!"

Oh, that was all right then. As long as the poor little thing could breathe as it was flung *bodily* around inside a bag as its owner jogged up and down the hills and paths of Ally Pally park...

"You still haven't told your parents?" I quizzed Kyra. "You promised you were going to do it yesterday, once your dad got home from work!"

"Well, I couldn't," Kyra mumbled petulantly. "Not after I'd had that row with Mum at lunchtime. I still wasn't talking to her last night!"

Good *grief*.

"Oi! You girls! Come on! No chatting – just running!" we suddenly heard Mr Bainbridge the gym teacher yell.

"Here!" said Kyra, shoving the sports bag at me. "Just look after Mushu till the race is over, Ally, and I'll work out what to do then!"

"No way!" I squeaked, aghast at how mental Kyra could be.

"Please, Ally!" Kyra whined, casting a worried glance in Mr Bainbridge's direction. "I'll owe you one! I'll – I'll catch up with that Feargal creep and get your notebook back off him for you!"

Before I could say "yes", "no", or "have you thought about getting your brain tested lately?" Kyra – and the rest of my mates – were off, tagging along with the last trickle of runners from this lap.

"She's mad ... and maddening," I mumbled to myself, as I took a bemused brown kitten out of the sports bag. Stuffing the empty bag into the hedge behind me, I held Mushu on my lap and wondered a) if it might like some of the Wotsits I'd been planning to buy, and b) if my day could get any more complicated.

I'll never know the answer to a), because the answer to b) turned out to be "yes", in the shape of Mrs Fisher.

"What have you got there, Ally Love?" she bellowed.

She was like a witch, she was, appearing out of nowhere like that, in a puff of poisoned smoke. Where'd she parked her broomstick?

"It's, um, a kitten," I mumbled, knowing that *somehow*, Mrs Fisher wasn't going to like this.

"Well, you can't sit there stroking kittens when you've got a job to do. Put it *down*."

"But I think it might be lost," I muttered, silently cursing Kyra for getting me into another predicament and making me lie all over again. I'd be a twitching, nervous wreck by the time the holidays started, thanks to her.

"Cats can find their own way home, Ally," Mrs Fisher stated bluntly. "Stop fussing over it and it'll soon wander off."

Eek! That's exactly what I didn't want this tiny scrap of cat to do. I had to think of a lie fast...

"Actually, I know whose kitten this is," I fibbed, feeling one side of my mouth begin to wibble up and down in a guilty spasm. "It belongs to a lady who lives just across the road – it must have got out on its own without her knowing. Can I, um, just go across and give it back to her?"

Mrs Fisher narrowed her eyes at me, smelling a lie, or old cabbage or something.

"All right, but be quick. I'll man this position for now."

And so she watched, arms folded, as I juggled kittens and crutches, struggling to my feet and starting the laborious hop across the street to Alice's house.

That Mrs Fisher ... she has a heart of pure *rock*.

"*Please* let Alice be in ... *please* let Alice be in..." I whispered to the wriggling kitten, as I felt Fish-Face's eyes bore into my back.

Luckily, as soon as I'd pressed the doorbell, I heard the pad of feet coming along the hall somewhere inside.

"Oh! Hello, you!" said a white-haired Alice, beaming me a big, welcoming smile. "It's Ally, isn't it? Can't forget that, since it's nearly the same name as mine! And named after the Palace, of course – we can't forget that, can we? Now, what have you got there?"

"Listen," I whispered, hoping Fish-Face didn't have the lampposts bugged, as well as direct links to every CCTV camera in the area. "Can you do me a huge, *huge* favour?"

Alice was already stroking Mushu, so that was a good sign.

"Could you look after this kitten for an hour or so?" I burbled on. "It's really complicated – I'll explain later. It's just that my teacher's over on the corner and she totally *hates* cats."

And schoolkids. And all living things in general, I think.

"Er … OK, my love," Alice gave me a puzzled glance, and took Mushu out of my arms. "Just an hour or so, you say?"

"Promise! Thank you *so* much!"

I must have had a look of sheer desperation on my face for Alice to go along with me so easily. Either that, or she'd taken one look at Fish-Face and immediately realized she was in the presence of a she-devil.

"Come on in, little one, and meet my cat. And let's get you some milk and something to eat, will we?" I heard Alice chatter as she pushed her front door closed.

Sadly, she was talking to Mushu and not me.

God, I wished I'd listened to everybody and stayed at home in my comfy, uncomplicated, pet-filled house today, instead of deciding it would be "fun" to come along here.

Note to myself: whenever my stupid brain comes up with an idea, never, *ever* encourage it. It'll only end in a throbbing ankle, a twitching face, a rumbly tummy and big, big trouble…

Chapter 11

ALIEN PETS

"Whaaa-*hey*! *Wheeee!*"

"Billy! *Don't!* You're scaring the dog!"

It was Wednesday evening, and me and Billy (and a growling dog under the bed) were in my attic bedroom. As a proper, *bona fide* invalid, I was reclining on my cloud-covered duvet, recovering from the day's Fun Run. (Make that *Non*-Fun Run, as far as I was concerned.)

Billy was in the middle of the room, swinging himself backwards and forwards on my crutches, like they were some excellent new ride at the fairground.

"Winslet? Scared? Give me a break!" snorted Billy. "If a ten-tonne truck was hurtling down a hill in her direction, Winslet wouldn't be scared. She'd just try to bite the *tyres* as they came straight for her!"

Billy.

Billy, Billy, Billy.

My so-called oldest mate had come round –

supposedly to cheer me up – and *so* far he'd only managed to eat most of the Cadbury's Celebrations box he'd brought with him *and* managed to bug me stupid.

You want a "for instance"? Well, he'd started laughing at my mummified leg as soon as I opened the door, then practically wet himself as he followed me hobbling two flights up to my room, and actually cried with laughter when I'd described the whole, hideous tripping-on-the-stage drama in all its gory detail.

"Yeah, but Winnie *really* doesn't like the crutches," I tried to tell Billy, as he lifted his feet off the carpet and swung some more. "I think she thinks they're some kind of alien pet life form trying to move in. She's getting very territorial."

"Huh?" Billy frowned.

At least I *presumed* he was frowning. It was hard to tell since his newest baseball cap was pulled down so low on his forehead.

"She's dragged her blanket and food bowl from downstairs and hidden them under my bed," I explained, not bothering to mention the loo brush, anonymous pink sock, nearly-empty anti-dandruff shampoo bottle and red electricity bill reminder that she'd dragged under my bed for comfort too.

"So, anyway," said Billy, swinging happily and

ignoring what I was saying about Winslet. "How did you get the kitten back?"

"I tripped Kyra up with my crutch when she passed on the third lap and told her if she didn't get right round to Alice's – with biscuits to say thank you – straight after the race finished, I would personally take an ad out in the local *Hornsey Journal* giving her mobile phone number out as a 24-hour pizza delivery service."

"Oh," Billy raised his eyebrows (as far as I could make out) under his cap. "And you got the kitten back OK?"

"OK-ish," I groaned. "It would have been better if it had stayed permanently with Alice, only her own cat kept hissing at it. At least she gave it proper cat food. At Kyra's, it's like a secret refugee cat, living on fresh air and Rolos, knowing Kyra."

"*'Like a kitten, in a sports bag, waiting to drowwwwwnnnnnn…'*" Billy began to sing, for no good reason that I could see.

"What are you on about?" I frowned at him, as the growling from under the bed got louder.

"It's a song! Or my version of it! By that band, The Verve, remember? From ages ago?" he grinned, like the idiot he was.

"Billy, shut up."

What was it with boys? Billy was as bad as Feargal,

in his own way. (And no, Kyra *hadn't* managed to wangle my journal back from him during the course of the Non-Fun Run. Oh, what a surprise...)

"You're as bad as Feargal," I said out loud.

"No I'm not!" Billy said, sounding slightly out-raged. "I'm your friend!"

"Yeah, but you laugh at me like he does!"

"Only 'cause I like you!" Billy frowned, looking a bit put-out.

"It's not the same, though, is it?" I pointed out, from my comfy, pillow-supported position. "You like me, and he doesn't!"

"He probably *fancies* you..." Billy grumbled.

I felt my face flush red as a baboon's bottom at Billy's ridiculous (and faintly alarming) suggestion.

"Billy! Don't be stupid!" I squeaked indignantly. "He's been horrible to me!"

"That's what you do sometimes, when you fancy a girl," Billy replied churlishly.

"No – you don't know what Feargal's *like*," I argued. "He does horrible things 'cause he thinks it's fun being mean. He and all his mates are trouble..."

"Like?"

"Like?" I repeated, as Billy swung between my crutches, with a low, rumbly echo of a growl going on under my bed.

"Like … Feargal and his mates are the tough lads in my year."

"Which means … they've done *what* exactly?" asked Billy, swooping and swinging.

"I dunno," I shrugged from my reclining position. "Everyone just says they're the tough lads, and that's … *it*."

"Which means they've done *nothing*," Billy grinned, swinging away. "If they were *really* bad, like joyriders or experts at nicking stuff, you'd have heard about it by now. But I know guys like that at *my* school; probably the toughest thing they've ever done is put chewing gum under the desks…"

Maybe Billy was right about Feargal and his meat-head mates.

I dunno.

But what *I* was right about was the fact that Winslet really, *really* hated those crutches, which was obvious once she came tearing out from beneath Billy's trainers and whatever else might get between her and those scary, invading, alien pets.

Ah, well – served him right for coming out with that wiffle about Feargal fancying me.

I mean, as *if*…

Chapter 12

THE PITTER-PATTER OF TINY PAWS

Call me a fool ("You're a fool, Ally Love!"), but I really do try to be optimistic about stuff.

You know, like maybe I'll come home for lunch one day and find Mum de-fleaing the cats or something ordinary (that doesn't involve her being thousands of kilometres away from us for years). Or that one day, I'll end up with boobs as nice as Linn's, living in a painted houseboat with geraniums in pots, listening to my husband Alfie telling me how gorgeous I am. That kind of stuff.

And – despite having the week from hell so far – I couldn't help feeling flutters of excitement about the end-of-term party tonight.

Oh, yes, it *is* humanly possible for me to stop worrying (about people seeing my knickers, having my journal stolen, having a leg that doesn't work, etc.) for five minutes at a time.

"So, Ally," said Salma, as she and Jen settled themselves into the desks right behind me, at the first lesson after lunch this Thursday.

☆(105)☆

"What?" I asked, leaning my crutches against the window and wriggling awkwardly down into my seat.

All around us, everyone was screeching chairs, thumping books out of bags on to the desks and trying to squeeze in a last bit of chatting, before Mr Matthews our French teacher made us shut up.

"Are you wearing your new cords tonight, Al?"

"Yeah, of course," I shrugged at Salma's question. "They go really well with the top Rowan's lend—"

Ah, now *there* was something to stress out about. I couldn't wear my new trousers, could I? Not unless I took the kitchen scissors to them and cut a stupid great chunk out of one leg so I could get it over my stupid great chunk of mummified *leg*.

Great.

Now I'd have to spend all my getting-ready time tonight trying to work out what on earth to put on instead. My school skirt? A *towel*?! Hmm ... *that*'d be nice with the heart-patterned T-shirt I'd been planning to wear.

"Is Sandie coming to the party?" asked Jen.

"She wants to, but her mum might not let her, since she's been off sick," I told the girls, over the back of my chair. "You know what her mum's like..."

Jen and Salma both rolled their eyes. *They* knew.

And were eternally grateful that their own mums didn't try to do stuff like physically frisk you to check that you were wearing a vest in front of *all* your mates when they'd turned up for a Girls' Video Night.

"Quieten down, now, you lot!" Mr Matthews boomed. "Books out – turn to page 73, where we left off last time. Oh, good *evening*, Miss Davies, nice of you to join us…"

"Sorry I'm late," muttered Kyra, zooming past Mr Matthews's desk and making a beeline for Sandie's vacant spot next to me.

I was just about to flick to whichever exciting French verbs lay on page 73, when I froze. Kyra was carrying the sports bag again. On an afternoon when we had zero sports lessons she could legitimately use it for.

Oh, no.

She hadn't.

Please tell me she hadn't…

"Don't say anything," Kyra mumbled loudly, reading my mind as she plonked herself down next to me. "There was nothing else I could do! I went home at lunchtime, and you'll never believe what happened with my horror of a mother!"

"You mean, you *didn't* tell your parents about Mushu last night, like you *promised* you were going to?" I hissed, casting a troubled eye over the ominously non-moving bag.

"It wasn't the right time!" Kyra shrugged, all innocence.

"Kyra, Ally, enough now," Mr Matthews said, shooting us a warning glance.

Kyra pulled a face at him as soon as he glanced away from us and continued with what she was saying, in a whisper. That is, a *Kyra* whisper, which is no whisper at all.

"But my mum knows about Mushu now!" she informed me. "She was noseying around in my room just before I arrived home. My God – we had the *worst* row! And she threatened to give Mushu away to the Cats' Protection League! So what could I do? I had to do *some*thing, so when she went to the loo, I put Mushu in my bag and scarpered back here!"

"Kyra! Ally! I won't tell you two again!" Mr Matthews frowned, even though I hadn't opened my mouth. Well, unless you count the fact that my jaw had dropped open at Kyra's amazingly limited grasp on reality.

"Kyra!" I murmured in the softest (yet angriest) voice, undercover of everyone rustling through their books. "You *can't* keep a kitten in a bag all afternoon!

"It's OK! Mushu'll just sleep! On the way here, I bought a tin of tuna and emptied it into the bag. It always dozes off after it's been fed!"

Yeah, dozes or dies from lack of oxygen.

(And I'd been wondering what the faint waft of fish had been all about...)

I couldn't help it – I didn't trust the fact that the bag was supposed to have airholes. I had to bend down under the desk and check for myself that Mushu was still in the land of the living. Tor would never forgive me if—

"Ally!" Mr Matthews bellowed, making me (ouch) wallop my head against the underside of the desk. "Would you kindly sit up, please! And Kyra, if I hear *one* more word out of you this afternoon, then I will have to— oh!"

The *oh!* was followed by giggles and *aaawww*s from the whole room, as Mushu, spotting a chink of light as I pulled at the bag's zip, slipped Houdini-style from its prison and skittered its way daintily across the classroom floor.

"*Voici! Un petit chat!*" giggled Jen, right behind us.

And thanks to that *petit chat*, and that not-so-*petit* pain in the bum that goes by the name of Kyra Davies, five minutes later all three of us (me, Kyra and Mushu) were hovering outside Mrs

Fisher's office, about to have our heads bitten off.

Yep, welcome to Day Four of my Week From Hell...

Chapter 13

HEY, THERE'S A FIRST TIME FOR EVERYTHING ... (URGH)

The end-of-day bell had just gone, and everyone in our year was happily zooming home to get ready for the big party. Or *nearly* everyone...

Me and Kyra had been given exactly five minutes leeway by Fish-Face: for Kyra, that meant going to check on Mushu, who'd spent the afternoon snoozling and boinging around in the janitor's big, walk-in broom cupboard; and for me, it meant a chance to hobble off and find Rowan, so that I could tell her to let Dad and Grandma know (urgh) that I wouldn't be home for another hour or so...

"Detention? *You?*" Rowan had pulled a face, which made her look more like a cartoon, what with all the mad spikes she'd waxed her fringe into today (for whatever Rowan-reason that was). "You've never had detention in your *life*, Ally!"

"I know," I winced, gripping the handles of my crutches till my knuckles went white with shame. "Listen, Ro, I've got to go. I've got to be in the library in about ten seconds' time or I get even *more* detention."

And so I'd left my sister, frowning after me, and hoppity-hopped my way at high speed towards the library, and Mrs Hawkins, the teacher who'd drawn the short straw and had to supervise the delinquents in detention today. Which included me. Arrrggghhhh!

Every *thunk!* of my crutches as I hobbled towards the library made my heart sink deeper, deeper, down, down and *deeper* into the hard-wearing, industrial, red lino of the corridor.

This was *awful*.

I'd got into more trouble at school this week than I had in the whole of the rest of my time at school (including primary) put together. I felt like a thug. And it was all down to Kyra and her nonfunctioning brain...

"Take a seat!" Mrs Hawkins ordered me, as soon as she spied me over the top of her slightly intimidating half-moon specs.

I gave her a pathetic, watery smile and steered my crutches in the direction of the rows of study desks in the centre of the room. There were plenty of people already there, grumpily and grudgingly doing their homework under Mrs Hawkins's hawkish gaze, but as far as I could see, there was no sign of Kyra. Not yet, anyway. There *were*, however, a couple of familiar (hooded) faces gawping at me from the back row – one pasty-white and gormless (Baz Meat-head) and one dark, quite good-looking but mean (Feargal O'Leary).

But, amazingly, there were no yelps of "Blue Bum", or annoying, sniggered *"Pffffttttt!"*s. Maybe neither Feargal or Baz Meat-head wanted their detention dragged out – whatever it was they'd done during the day to warrant it. Frankly, I didn't care. All *I* wanted was a) for this whole, hideous experience to be over as quickly as possible, b) for this whole, hideous experience to be as painless and hassle-free as possible, and c) for Kyra to hurry up and join me.

But ten minutes later and halfway through my (extra) French homework, there was *still* no sign of Kyra. It was only when Mrs Hawkins got up and strolled up and down between us all at the desks that I decided to – politely – take a chance and ask if she knew where Kyra might be.

"Kyra?" Mrs Hawkins squinted at me, while I was sure I heard someone muttering "Where's your parrot, Long John Silver?" in the background, followed by a stifled *"Pffftttttt!"*

"Yes, Kyra," I nodded shyly. "Kyra Davies. We both got detention tonight for the same reason."

"Ah, Kyra *Davies*!" Mrs Hawkins announced in recognition, like she'd been scanning her memory banks to see who I could have meant when I mentioned Kyra. (It couldn't have been *that* troublingly hard – count them up and there is exactly *one* girl called Kyra in our *entire* school.)

"Yes, Kyra," I repeated stupidly, hoping that the not-very-bright Mrs Hawkins might give me a clue as to where my detention buddy might be.

"Yes, I spoke to Kyra. She was excused from doing detention tonight, because she had to deal with the ... er ... kitten situation," explained Mrs Hawkins. "Her detention has been deferred to another day."

Oh, *nice* one, Kyra. There was only one more day of school left this term, which meant that by the time next term rolled around – the start of a whole new school year – *no one* would remember that she had an unused detention hanging over her head.

So Kyra gets to go swanning off with Mushu, I growled inside my own head, *while I have to sit here in the company of drongos like Feargal and Baz for something that wasn't even my fault!*

Just as I thought that growly, resentful thought, and *just* as Mrs Hawkins wandered off to spy on more detention homeworkers, a crumpled ball of paper *ping*ed off my ear and landed with a plop on the desk in front of me.

The paper had marks on it; handwriting actually. *My* handwriting actually, I noticed, as I unravelled it.

Q: *What's brown and sticky? A: A stick!*

Hey, it had seemed like a good (lousy) joke when I wrote it down in the privacy of my own bedroom, in the privacy of my own journal, on Sunday night.

But right now, it seemed about as funny as a torn ligament.

I knew Feargal O'Leary had ripped that page out of the notebook he'd somehow wangled from me. And right now, if I had a brown sticky stick in my possession, I knew *exactly* whose nose I'd like to ram it up...

Chapter 14

KYRA'S TEMPORARY GIFT...

Well, you've got to look on the bright side (even if my life didn't seem to have much of a bright side this week).

I was spared Grandma's disappointed, disapproving looks when I finally got home – she and Stanley were going out somewhere fancy that night, so she'd left us mounds of salad, a giant dish of lasagne and a list of instructions on how to heat up the lasagne and remove it from the oven without burning the skin off our limbs. (She thinks of everything, she really does.)

"Hey! They let you out on parole!" grinned Rowan, pausing in the hallway and leaning – arms crossed – up against the wall where the stairs were.

"Yeah, I got out early for good behaviour," I joked wryly, clattering the front door shut with a crutch.

And it was true – I had got out early for good behaviour, along with nearly everyone else. Because it was the second last day before the holidays, Mrs

Hawkins – full of the milk of human kindness since she was looking forward to six weeks of kid-free bliss – told us we could leave, only half an hour into the hour-long detention. That didn't include Feargal and Baz Meat-head though; Mrs Hawkins had caught them listening to their CD Walkmans instead of doing homework and made them stay till the bitter end.

Pity, really – I'd almost worked up enough courage to confront Feargal after detention finished. I'd been toying with using a pincer movement and trapping him by the neck with my crutches till he gave me back what was left of my journal.

"So how was it?" asked Rowan, unaware that a curious cat that wasn't Colin had stuck its nose through the bannisters at head level and was at this moment warily sniffing her wax spikes of fringe.

"It was…" I pretended to muse, "…let's see … *dull*. Yep, that's the word."

"Oh, by the way, while I remember," Rowan interjected. "Sandie called."

"Did she say if she's coming to the party tonight?" I asked, wriggling myself – one sleeve at a time – out of my blazer.

"Yes, she's definitely up for it," Rowan nodded, making the waxed spikes bounce back and forward. "But she says she's really worried about her nose."

"Her nose?" I frowned.

"She says it's bright red and scaly, 'cause she's been blowing it so much this week," Rowan grinned. "God, what are you two going to look like tonight? Sandie with her beacon of a nose and you with your crutches and gammy leg? It's going to look like party night at the Whittington Hospital!"

Rowan laughed at her own *hilarious* observations, oblivious to the fact that the cat that wasn't Colin had now stuck its paw through the bannister and was batting at her bobbing clump of fringe.

"Dad in?" I asked her, ignoring her feeble attempts at humour at my expense. (Feargal, Billy, now Rowan … honestly, everyone seemed to think that my mummified leg was some big, bandaged joke.)

"Yeah, he just got back from work. He's out in the garden hanging out— *ooow!* Eddie! Don't *do* that!"

I left Rowan rubbing at the claw marks in her scalp and hopped through the hallway, into the kitchen, and over to the back door.

There was Dad, wearing his ever-present jeans, T-shirt and red checked shirt, hanging up his overalls on the washing line and whistling Elvis's "Return to Sender".

OK, so looking on the bright side again, at least he didn't seem too traumatized by the news of the appalling behaviour of Love Child No. 3. (Me.)

"Hey, Ally Pally!" he called out cheerily, alerted to my presence by Winslet growling at the intruding metal alien pets. "How was jail?"

Oh, phew. He was making jokes about it. He really wasn't mad at me. I'd have rushed over and hugged him, if it wasn't for the fact that I'd fall over if I let go of my crutches.

"It was all right. Just had to do my homework, that's all," I shrugged.

"Rowan says Kyra landed you two in a spot of bother, then?" he grinned.

"You could say that," I grinned back.

Then I noticed a weird thing – Rolf wandering happily across the garden with a bunch of clothes pegs pinned on to his fur.

"Oh, *that*," said Dad, following my gaze. "That was just Tor helping me with the washing."

"Ahh…" I nodded, as everything made (sort of) sense.

"Anyway, don't worry about the detention business, Ally," Dad smiled, finishing with his overalls and sticking a handful of unused pegs back in the peg bag on the grass, which Winslet was chewing (while keeping a wary eye on the aliens on either side of me). "I know you're a good kid. And I was *always* getting detention at school."

"Were you?" I said in surprise. "I never knew that! What did you do?"

"Mostly, I wore clothes that weren't proper school uniform – drainpipe trousers, '50s style brothel-creeper shoes, that kind of thing," said Dad, walking towards the back door, then standing aside to let me hop ahead of him. "And badges – my school didn't allow badges. Well, actually, they didn't allow badges with swear words on them and I had a couple of those, 'cause of some of the punk music I was listening to."

I like it when Dad smiles (and he does it a lot, which is nice). He's got a skinny face that crinkles and dimples in this really cute way when he's grinning.

"So, you're a bad 'un like your Dad, huh?" he teased me, nudging me with one elbow, till I wobbled on my crutches.

"Hey, Ally!" I heard Linn's voice call out breezily from behind me in the kitchen. "Are *you* in trouble with Grandma!"

I'd like to say I spun round to face her, but in my current predicament that would have been impossible. Let's just say I did a three-point turn.

"Is she really mad at me getting detention?" I winced.

"She's not too thrilled about that, but no – that's

not the problem," Linn smirked, as she began to set the table.

"Linn, don't tease her…" said Dad.

"What is it?" I asked, looking from Dad back to Linn. "What's Grandma mad at me for?"

"*That*," Linn nodded in the direction of Tor, whom I hadn't noticed playing contentedly in the corner of the room.

Playing contentedly … *with a kitten*.

"Mushu!" I gasped.

"Isn't he lovely?" Tor beamed up at me. "Kyra said we could keep him for *ages*!"

I glanced around at Dad.

"Don't ask me – it was just Grandma and Tor who were in when Kyra turned up," Dad shrugged.

"Tor, what did she say exactly?" I quizzed my brother.

"She said the teacher was mad at her … and you."

Don't remind me…

"Yeah, but what did she bring Mushu here for?" I asked. (Like I didn't know. Like me and my family didn't have "Suckers for Animals" written on our foreheads.)

"She said her mummy is mad at her too," Tor replied blithely, wafting a feathery cat wand back and forth across the floor as Mushu pounced on it with its (sorry, *his*, as Tor seemed to have discovered) tiny paws.

"I got in just after Kyra had left," Linn took up the story. "Grandma said Kyra spun her this tale about having nowhere else to go with the cat. Grandma tried to tell her we've got no vacancies at the pet motel, but Kyra kept begging her."

So, while I was stuck in the school library, Kyra was round my house, emotionally blackmailing my family into taking Mushu off her hands. No wonder Grandma wasn't happy. She isn't the world's greatest animal lover at the best of times (they do too much hair-shedding and licking for her liking), and Kyra was really out of order, trying to dump another small mouth to feed on us. Why couldn't she take Mushu round to Claire Easton's, for goodness' sake? It was *her* cousin's cat who'd given birth to it, after all…

"Grandma says you've got to have a word with Kyra and sort this out," Linn continued. "Since she's your friend."

My friend? Oh, *yeah*? Who says…?

Chapter 15

HOPALONG AND SNOTTY

With her long, tumbly, dark hair and hooded cat eyes, Salma can look slinky and sexy in just about *any*thing (OK, maybe not a rubbish Palace Gates school blazer). But tonight she looked particularly gorgeous in a tight, black, long-sleeved top, dark red skirt and knee-high boots.

Jen was wearing this brilliant cap-sleeved T-shirt with "Sugarbabe" written on the front in diamanté; Kellie had on this cute little chiffony dress in an aqua sort of colour that went really well with her dark skin; and Chloe was decked out in wide-leg jeans with a gold-coloured halterneck.

They all looked great, my mates, as they danced non-stop in the darkened, light-spangled school hall, pausing now and then to wave madly over at me and Sandie, propping up the far wall like the pair of saddos we were.

I felt a bit weird, if you want to know the truth. Not 'cause of what I was wearing – Rowan had done me proud, lending me not only her heart-patterned top but her long denim skirt too – but because of other stuff.

Mainly…

1) I couldn't dance, and I *love* to dance. It was like having a curry delivered to your house when you're starving and then being told you're not allowed to eat it – not the tiniest nibble on a popadum or anything.

2) I felt sad that the usual getting-ready-for-a-party-together thing hadn't happened with me and my friends. Well, it did – for Chloe, Kellie, Salma and Jen, who'd all piled round Kel's house before they came here tonight. *I* couldn't make it (since it was tiring enough just to hobble around to the school), *Sandie* couldn't make it (she was too busy getting fed last-minute, germ-blasting vitamins by her mum) and Kyra *should* have made it, but didn't turn up at Kellie's at all.

3) Where was Kyra? I know I'd been mad at her ever since I found out that Mushu had become our lodger (I'd tried to phone her mobile but she had it switched off, and I was too much of a chicken to phone her house), but right now, I had a funny feeling that something was up, with a capital U. Kyra would never miss an opportunity to show off if she could help it.

4) Something I couldn't quite put my finger on

was bugging me. What it was exactly, I couldn't tell you, but there was definitely *something* going on in this big darkened hall that was working my nerves...

"Hey, have you noticed?" said Sandie, digging yet another paper tissue out of her dainty embroidered bag.

Poor babe, she might as well have had a tap installed in the middle of her face, her little red nose was running so much. She looked like she might have a fever too – or maybe she'd just overdone the "healthy glow" of blusher on her milk-white face.

"Noticed what?" I asked, readjusting the arm-rests of my crutches a little so that they didn't dig in so badly.

"Just keep looking at me." She widened her blue eyes at me. "It's Feargal O'Leary – he's staring over at you. *Really* hard. Check it out – he's over by the stage, by the DJ's decks. Don't make it obvious!"

Like I would. The idea of gazing anywhere near the stage made me feel ill; maybe it looked different with all those fancy banks of disco lights piled on it, but it was still the scene of my most embarrassing moment *ever*. Er, so far.

Sandie gazed down strategically at her pink and white trainers, giving me the opportunity to glance casually around, like I was just innocently scanning the room.

Sure enough – Feargal O'Leary was staring at me. And not sniggering, which was odd. His meat-head mates were in their usual hooded huddle, chattering or bitching or whatever, but Feargal was standing to one side of them, elbows resting on the stage, foot up on the wall, staring.

Uh-oh… This was my number 4) on the list: the certain something that was making me feel weird. Call me spooky or whatever, but somehow I'd just *known* I was being stared at.

But why? It was more unnerving seeing him come over all serious than it was to see him laughing at me. What did it mean? What was this about? What was Feargal planning? Was he going to kick my crutches away from under me when I wasn't looking?

"God, here you are!" Kyra suddenly appeared panting by our sides.

She was wearing the new trousers and scary, stripy one-shouldered top she'd bought on Saturday, I noticed. And her new sandals. Which were covered in mud, just like her pink-painted toes…

Instead of ranting at her about detention/skiving detention/taking advantage of my family, I took one look at Kyra's slightly ramshackle appearance and could only say, "Are you OK?"

"No." Kyra shook her head of freed-up, wild curls madly. "I've been grounded."

"What for?" frowned Sandie, her eyes wandering over Kyra's chest, as Kyra yanked up the side of her top that was slipping treacherously low.

"I got a cat. Mum thinks I'm the anti-Christ. That sort of thing," Kyra shrugged casually, although it took one peek at her darting eyes to see that she felt anything but casual.

"Did you end up fighting with your mum again? When she found out you'd sneaked out with Mushu at lunchtime?" I asked, trying to get a handle on what was going on.

"Fight? You'd think I'd robbed my dad's bank or something!" Kyra replied agitatedly, ruffling the front of her hair with her hand. "It was all 'You have no respect for us!' and 'You can't go around just doing what you like!'"

"But wait a minute, Kyra – if you're grounded, how come you're here?" Sandie sniffled, dabbing at her sandpapered nose.

"I climbed out of my bedroom window on to the kitchen roof, then got down on to our wheelie bin and sneaked off through the rose bushes." Kyra shrugged, instantly reminding me of her mountain goat act the time we watched Chazza's band playing from the elegant viewpoint of the top of a wall in a smelly back alley. (Classy, huh?)

"Which explains the mud," I muttered, letting go of a crutch and pointing to her feet.

"Huh?" frowned Kyra, gazing down at her pink-painted tootsies. "Oh, no! God, what a state I look!"

"Here…" said Sandie, passing Kyra a tissue.

"Thanks," Kyra mumbled, picking up one foot and vainly rubbing at it. "Nah… I'd better nip to the loos and try and wash this stuff off."

She'd just turned to leave us, when something stopped her. A pang of guilt, perhaps?

"Listen – I'm sorry about dumping Mushu on you, Ally, but I didn't know what else to do." She batted the long lashes of her almond eyes at me appealingly.

That Bambi trick might work on boys, but it *sure* didn't work on me…

"Why can't you give Mushu to Claire Easton?" I pointed out.

"Can't. Asked her already but her dad's allergic to fur. And I've got no way of taking it down to Brighton to her cousin."

"Well, you can't leave him with us permanently, Kyra," I told her, trying my best to seem stern (hard to do when you're hunched up over a pair of crutches).

"'Him'?" Kyra blinked at me.

"Mushu's a boy," I informed her. "Tor checked."

"Oh. Anyway, don't worry – I know you can't keep him. I'll... I'll figure something out. Promise."

Hmm. I didn't think much of Kyra's promises and I think she knew it.

"Honest, Ally! I *do* promise!" she said earnestly. "And I'll do anything you want in return. Anything!"

I narrowed my eyes at her, thought for a second, then wrinkled my nose and muttered, "Nah!"

"No! Go on!" she encouraged me. "What were you going to ask?"

"It's something you promised you'd do before, but you didn't," I told her.

"What? What didn't I do?"

"At the Fun Run yesterday – you promised you'd get my journal back off Feargal and you never did!" I pointed out accusingly.

"You never gave me the chance!" Kyra defended herself. "You tripped me up with your crutch and then frog-marched me to the shop to buy Jammy Dodgers for that old lady who was looking after Mushu!"

True.

"Still, a promise is a promise." I stared meaning-fully at her.

"OK, OK!" Kyra held her hands palms-up. "I'll speak to him tonight. I absolutely and totally promise. I'll go and find him as soon as I've got this muddy gloop off my shoes and my feet."

"You don't have too look hard to find him," sniffled Sandie. "He's over there, by the— *oh*. He *was* over by the stage."

But Feargal wasn't there now, *or* any of his meat-heads. Maybe they'd all found the end-of-term party too juvenile for them and pootled off to do something more exciting like hang around on street corners and moodily kick empty cans at each other.

If it hadn't been for the fact that I really wanted my journal back, I would have kind of hoped that was the case.

"Back in a minute," mumbled Kyra, striding off in the direction of the loos, while firmly grasping the one, downward-slipping side of her scary, stripy top. (She should have listened to Grandma's tip about the safety pin...)

Kyra's minutes, like Kyra's whispers, are not like other people's. Half an hour must have passed and there was still no sign of her.

Meanwhile, lots had been going on with me and Sandie. Lots of *nothing*, that is. Sandie had tried to join Chloe and the others for a dance, but come back and rejoined me and the wall halfway through the record 'cause her nose kept running. Then I'd tried to hobble to the buffet with her, but it was too crowded for a girl in my precariously un-balanced state, so Sandie went off on her own to get us both some food, and came back with a cold sausage roll, some coleslaw and a spoon, explaining that they'd run out of practically everything – including forks. Then Jen, Kellie, Salma and Chloe took it in turns to rush off the dancefloor to tell us what a brilliant night they were having and how many times they'd been asked to dance by cute boys (oh, goody). Probably the best fun (and that's not saying much) was when Sandie and I decided to make up rubbish nicknames for each other: I was Lady Hopalong of Hornsey, and she was the Marquise of Snotsville; Hopalong and Snotty to our closest friends, i.e. each other.

Pathetic, huh?

"I think I'll go to the loo. Coming?" asked Sandie.

"You bet," I nodded enthusiastically.

Well, anything to get away from the wall we'd been propping up for the last hour and a half.

"Maybe we'll find Kyra," Sandie suggested over

her shoulder, as she cleared a path through everyone, so that Lady Hopalong of Hornsey could pass.

"Maybe," I replied, breathlessly, trying to keep up with her.

"Maybe she's got hold of that Feargal lad!" she suggested, holding open the heavy door that led out of the heaving, noisy hall into the cool, practically empty corridor. The sudden, bright, unsubtle lighting out here bounced painfully off the back of my eyeballs. (So much for a week of fun – it was a week of pain.)

"Maybe," I answered her, unconvinced. Knowing her, Kyra was probably at my house right now, handing round hand-made chocolate cake to members of my family, while getting Dad to sign a legal document stating we'd keep Mushu for life.

"Listen!" whispered Sandie, just as we approached the doors to the girls' loos. "Isn't that Kyra ... laughing?"

She was right. I'd recognize that dirty cackle anywhere. And it was coming from ... the boys' loos.

Me and Sandie both stared at each other, then stared at the door with the matchstick bloke sign on it, then stared at each other again.

"Should we?" she asked nervously.

I wrinkled my nose till it hurt. The idea of

barging into the boys' toilets and getting caught made me feel ill. But I was practically bursting with curiosity to see what Kyra was playing at.

"C'mon!" I said, taking my courage (and crutches) in hand, and hopping over to the swing door.

Snotty and I peered through a five-centimetre gap at first, just to check we weren't going to give ourselves, and any weeing boys, a nasty shock. But the loos were currently empty of anyone – except Feargal and Kyra, standing by the sinks sharing a) a laugh, and b) a cigarette.

Um, excuse me...?

"Kyra!" I squeaked indignantly, as the door swung closed behind me and Sandie. "You don't smoke!"

And you don't laugh and joke with someone who appears to be my sworn enemy either.

The smiles, I noticed, had suddenly slipped from Kyra and Feargal's faces. Wow – we must *really* have given them a fright. Obviously they hadn't been expecting—

"What on *earth*'s going on here! All of you – out of here now!" growled Mrs All-Seeing Fisher from the doorway. "Smoking in the boys' lavatories indeed!"

Er ... not *all* of us. I mean, *technically*, yes, me and Sandie *were* in the lads' loos, but we certainly weren't *smoking*.

"But Mrs Fish—"

"Save it, Ally Love! I want to see you all after assembly tomorrow in my office – is that understood?"

All *I* understood was that this week had definitely won first prize for being the Crummiest Week Of My Life.

Cold sausage roll, anyone…?

Chapter 16

JOY TO THE WORLD!

It was Friday morning. It was only a few short hours till lunchtime ... and freedom. But first we had to get through one assembly and three lessons. (Not to mention a torture session with Fish-Face, if you happened to be me, Sandie, Kyra or Feargal flippin' O'Leary.)

"...and of course, this last year, Palace Gates School has had an excellent academic *blah-de-blah*. But there's always room for *blah, blah...*"

Mr Bashir – he's dead nice for a headmaster and everything, but he doesn't half make boring speeches. He should put more jokes in during assembly, or do a tap dance halfway through – *that*'d keep everyone's attention.

"...so when you come back after the holidays, I hope you will all continue to *blah, blah, blah...*"

"He fancies you," Kyra muttered.

She wasn't talking about Mr Bashir, before you go jumping to any weird conclusions.

"Kyra, he does *not* fancy me," I hissed back.

God, she was as bad as Billy – he'd said that too, without ever having set eyes on Feargal O'Leary.

"He does *so* fancy you."

Aaargghhh!

"Kyra! You are *so* making this up! If Feargal fancies me, I'm a *frog*."

"Ribbit… Ribbit," Kyra ribbitted, with her eyes glued to the stage and a wicked grin on her face.

Ooh, she can wind me up so much.

"Kyra, you have *no* proof that he fancies me," I pointed out, in a teeny-tiny whisper. "He didn't say anything like that to you last night – you said so yourself!"

She and Billy … they both had vivid imaginations, that was for sure.

"Yeah, but I just *know* it…" Kyra turned and smirked knowingly at me.

OK, so here's what happened the night before, right *after* Mrs Fisher had put her hex on us (old witch that she is). I don't mean the bit about Sandie bursting into tears and me having to reassure her that getting an unwarranted and undeserved tongue-lashing off Fish-Face was all right (when I had my doubts). And I don't mean when Chloe and Kellie tried to cheer me up by stealing my crutches, bodily lifting me on to the dancefloor and spinning me around to Abba's

"Dancing Queen". I'm talking about Kyra telling us how her conversation with Feargal had gone. And according to her, it went something like this...

KYRA (on the way to the loo to wash her muddy tootsies, via many chats with many people): "Oi, Feargal! I want a word with you!"

FEARGAL (coming out of the boys' loos): "Oh, yeah? What about?"

KYRA (pointing at the girls' loos): "In here; in private."

FEARGAL (pointing at the boys' loos): "Well, in *here*, in private. If you can handle it."

KYRA (thinking for about a milli-second, and then following him, 'cause she can never resist a dare): "I can handle it!"

FEARGAL (by the sinks, as he frightens two boys away by having Kyra in tow): "Fag?"

KYRA (feeling rebellious after her monumental row at home): "Yeah, OK."

[Feargal lights a cigarette and passes it to Kyra; Kyra pretends to inhale, and passes it straight back.]

FEARGAL: "So ... what's the deal?"

KYRA (coughing slightly): "The deal is ... Ally Love's notebook."

FEARGAL (passing the cigarette back to Kyra): "Yeah? What about it?"

KYRA (tries to pretend to take another drag, but accidentally does and ends up hiccuping and coughing some more): "She ... *cough, cough, urp* ... wants it back."

FEARGAL: "Yeah?"

KYRA: "Yeah. *Cough ... cough...*"

FEARGAL: "Well, maybe I want to hold on to it for a while."

KYRA: "*Cough...* Why?"

FEARGAL: "Well, maybe I want to write something in it."

KYRA: "Yeah? Like what?"

FEARGAL: "Maybe a poem. Y'know, *'There once was a teacher called Fish-Face—'*"

[Kyra starts sniggering as soon as he starts his so-called "poem", but Feargal doesn't get any further with it, 'cause Kyra's sniggers turn into a full-on coughing fit.]

FEARGAL (with a smirk on his face): "You've, um, never smoked before, have you?"

KYRA (trying to look indignant, then launching into another telltale coughing fit): "*Cough, cough, cough, urp...* Yes, I have! *Cough, cough, cough, urp...* OK! No, I haven't! Ha, ha, ha, ha, ha, ha..."

[Cue me and Sandie arriving, closely followed by the Evil Fish-Faced One.]

"Ally!" Sandie nudged me in the ribs, suddenly. "Are you listening to this?"

I stopped reminiscing about last night's events (and stopped glaring black looks in Kyra's direction) long enough to turn my attention to the stage and Mr Bashir. Who right this minute was gesturing at Mrs Fisher to be upstanding, while a wishy-washy patter of applause was emitted from a few fellow teachers. (Hmm, it seemed like she was about as popular with the staff as she was with the pupils ... i.e. not at all, thank you very much.)

"Yes!" beamed Mr Bashir. "It's sad, but true... Mrs Fisher *will* be leaving us as from today, to take up a new post at a different school next term. Let's hear it for Mrs Fisher!"

I'm sure Mr Bashir meant it in the nicest, possible way ... but the rest of us didn't. As Fish-Face got uncomfortably to her feet, the noisy waves of applause (not just from our year – whom she tortured as Year Head – but from everyone in school who'd had the misfortune to cross her path) was positively deafening. It was the best news every person in school could hear; the best end-of-term present we could get.

Oh, joy to the world! Hallelujah! My hands were aching from clapping so hard. But who cared?

Honestly, it was like a dream … the end of *beautiful* ends to a totally hideous week…

"Picnic on Ally Pally this afternoon to celebrate?" Chloe said to my line-up of buddies.

"YES!" said me, Sandie, Kyra, Salma, Jen and Kellie in blissed-out reply.

Hey, maybe this week was turning out OK, after all.

You've got to be grateful for small mercies, haven't you? Specially when those mercies involved Mrs Fisher vacating the premises.

Oh, happy day!

If only Feargal O'Leary wasn't staring over at me again in a really weird way…

Chapter 17

PETS ON PROTEST

"Cheers!!" Jen called out, and we all clattered our cans of Diet Coke together.

"The best bit," giggled Kellie, while grabbing a Pringle from the opened tube, "*had* to be Mrs Fisher's face when Mr Bashir said that thing about the amnesty!"

"Yeah – it was like taking sweets away from a little kid!" Kyra laughed.

Oh, yes. How gutted was Fish-Face when Mr Bashir put the kibosh on any last-minute torturing she had planned? "Mrs Fisher, I know you're very committed to your responsibilities, but as this is your last day, I think you should be excused from any tiresome duties," Mr Bashir had announced. "So if any of you out there were due to see Mrs Fisher for disciplinary reasons this morning, consider yourselves reprieved. And try to behave better next term!"

Everyone started laughing when he said that (told you he should do more jokes at assembly).

Everyone, that is, except Mrs Fisher, who only managed a wan, fake smile. Unlike me, Sandie and Kyra, who couldn't wipe the grins of relief off our faces. We were off the hook! Free to snore our way through the next three classes till the end-of-school/beginning-of-holidays bell rang!

And now here we were – me and my bunch of best mates – sitting in the sunshine up on the grassy banks of Alexandra Palace, happily picnicking on highly un-nutritious cheese-and-Pringle-filled rolls. (Recipe: take one giant bread roll fresh from the baker's shop, slap on a Kraft individual cheese slice and sprinkle liberally with Sour Cream and Chive Pringles. Serving suggestion: stuff in your mouth. Preferably *without* stray blades of grass.)

"But you know something? I still can't believe you were smoking last night," Salma narrowed her eyes at Kyra.

"I *told* you," Kyra said indignantly, as she tugged off her school tie, "I wasn't smoking *really*! I was just doing it 'cause I was still angry with my mum and dad."

"Wow, you *really* showed them!" giggled Kellie. "Pretending to smoke in a boys' toilet – they must be *really* sorry for grounding you now!"

Kyra stuck her tongue out at that obvious dollop of sarcasm. Of *course* it was a stupid way to get back at her parents. But then, her parents knew nothing *about* her smoking. In fact they knew nothing about her sneaking out to the party the night before, since she'd sneaked back in exactly the same way three hours later...

"Hey, Kyra, and what about you getting all friendly with O'Leary, too?!" snickered Chloe. "How *cosy*!"

Kyra was looking slightly bugged. It's funny how she likes winding people up, but isn't very good at being on the receiving end.

"Look, it's not *me* he fancies ... it's Ally!"

"Don't start that rubbish again, Kyra!" I growled at her, waving my filled roll menacingly in her face. (That's how mean I am – armed with a bread roll and dangerous.)

"Yes, Kyra, but *you* were the one who was hanging out with one of the toughest lads in our year – not Ally!" Sandie pointed out, coming to my rescue (thank you very much).

"He is *not* tough. Neither are his mates. It's all just an act!" Kyra shrugged.

"Oh, yeah? And you know this for a fact, do you?" Chloe challenged her. "You think he's OK after having a two-second conversation with him?"

Hey, Kyra suspected him of fancying me after that two-second conversation, so it didn't surprise me if she'd now convinced herself that he was practically a saint. (Yeah, a saint who nicks people's journals...)

"Yes, I think he's OK. I think he's pretty friendly and funny actually," Kyra stated defiantly. "And he's pretty cute-looking, too."

"Whhhoooo-OOOOO-ooooooo!" we all crooned in unison.

"I didn't mean I *fancied* him!" Kyra yelled above us all. "I'm just saying he's pretty cute!"

But no one was paying much attention to her protests – we were all giggling too much. Hysteria was catching up with us through sheer tiredness after the party, sheer elation at the news of Fish-Face's departure and sheer *wheeeeee!*ness at the idea of being on holiday at last.

Kyra could see she wasn't going to win, so she stuck her sunglasses on her little snub nose, and lay back down to sunbathe till we all ran out of giggles. Which took some time, let me tell you.

"Hey, isn't there a fair on in Priory Park this weekend?" she asked two minutes later, once the rest of us finally got our breath back and stopped choking on our rolls. (Not an attractive sight.)

"Think there is," Jen spluttered. "There've been signs up all over the place."

"Well, why don't we go?" Kyra suggested,

propping herself up on her elbows. "Tonight, I mean. To celebrate."

"Yeah, let's!" said Chloe enthusiastically, as we all nodded in agreement.

"But will your parents let you out?" I teased Kyra.

"Of course," she smiled back lazily. "I served my punishment last night, didn't I?"

"*No!*" Sandie frowned, missing the irony dripping from Kyra's words.

"Yeah, but my parents don't *know* I sneaked out," she shrugged at Sandie. "And what they don't know doesn't hurt them!"

And that, ladies and gentlemen, boys and girls, is a perfect example of Kyra logic.

"Uh, Kyra, by the way..." I suddenly remembered to ask. "When exactly are you going to sort out the problem of Mushu?"

Acting like she hadn't heard me, Kyra smiled round at our other friends and said brightly, "Anyone want a kitten...?"

When I finally clattered my way into the kitchen, after taking about three days to hobble home from the picnic in the park, I had this spooky feeling that something wasn't quite right.

I glanced around, trying to figure out what it was

exactly, but everyone was smiling, everyone was happy. Was I just going slightly mad? (After the week I'd had and the painkillers I'd taken, I wouldn't have been *wildly* surprised.)

"Hi, Ally!" Linn smiled at me, dragging her eyes away from the unadulterated cuteness happening on the kitchen table. (I think she'd have been better off keeping an eye on what she was doing – ironing while looking at something else is a risky business.)

"Oh, hello, Ally, dear!" smiled Grandma, also absorbed in the cuteness.

And the cuteness consisted of one formerly brown kitten, which was now mostly cream-coloured, sitting beside a saucer and a puddle of milk in the middle of the kitchen table.

"He doesn't seem to have got the hang of the fact that he's supposed to *drink* the milk, not *wear* it!" Linn giggled, as a gently purring Mushu sat contentedly, with droplets of milk plopping off his mini whiskers and sploshing into the milk puddle he was more or less soaking up through his fur.

"Don't move!" came Tor's voice from over on the other side of the table. He had a camera pointed at Mushu, ready to capture the milky moment.

"Quick, Tor!" Grandma urged. "That shot'll be perfect!"

Perfect.

That word rattled around my head for a second, and then I realized two strange things about this whole scene going on in my kitchen:

a) Grandma was acting totally out of character – why wasn't she shooing Mushu off the table, like she normally does with the cats (and the occasional dog/rabbit/iguana)? And why wasn't she snapping on her Marigolds and rushing over to wipe away the milky mess? Usually, it only takes one stray cat hair to get her blasting Dettol anti-bacterial spray into the atmosphere.

b) Speaking of pet hairs, where *were* all the pets? There's always a dog or a cat or three hovering around in the kitchen. It is, after all, the warmest, busiest, *foodiest* room in the whole house. But right now, the only animal around was the fun-size furball on the table.

"Where's Rolf? Where's Colin? Or any of the rest of them?" I asked out loud.

"Haven't you noticed? They're all on strike. Pets on protest!" Linn said breezily.

"Huh?" I frowned, suddenly spotting – sure enough – a grumpy-looking couple of cats that weren't Colin hunkered down outside on the garden wall.

"Since this one arrived," Linn enlightened me,

pointing the iron she was holding at Mushu, "they've all gone in a huff, never coming near him. I think they think he's too posh for them, being part Siamese. They've probably all got inferiority complexes, since they're all bargain-basement, reject pets!"

Linn was only having a laugh, and it *was* hard to resist something as adorable as Mushu, but it didn't seem right...

Without anyone noticing (amazing, really, considering the random clanking noises I was making), I hopped my way out of the kitchen, along the hall and into the living room.

"*Pssssss-wwwwwwwssss!*" I called out, in the international cat language of the world, to the seemingly empty room.

A slight rustle came from behind the furthest away armchair. Manoeuvring myself past the sofa, past the beanbag, past the coffee table, over to that part of the room, I peered around the chair and found a soulful-looking Rolf, curled up with Colin.

"Hey, guys!" I whispered, struggling to lower myself down without making my ankle hurt any more than it was already hurting.

My face was within licking distance, but Rolf's doggy mouth stayed firmly closed, his scruffy chin resting forlornly on his paws.

"Are you jealous of that little kitten, huh?" I cooed softly, tickling both of them around the ears. "Jealous that it's cuter than you, Rolf? Jealous that it's got more legs than you, Colin?"

But I knew why they were *really* jealous. Much as everyone in my family loved the pets (Grandma excluded), Tor was chief zookeeper here, doling out love and attention to all his vast furry/feathery/scaly brood. But over-excitement at the arrival of Mushu seemed to have made him neglect his general duties in the hugging department.

"C'mere, you two," I muttered, scooping Colin up for a cuddle, and then affectionately ruffling the sticky-up spikes of fur on Rolf's head.

Our animals might be a little on the wonky side – not exactly perfect pedigree pets. But even with all their missing legs, bent tails, bitten ears and anti-social behaviour (yes, *you*, Winslet; not forgetting Mad Max the psycho hamster), wonky as they were, they were part of our wonky, not-so-perfect family. And it upset me to see them out of sorts.

That was it. I knew I couldn't rely on Kyra to sort this (or *anything*) out. Today, my head was still too swirly from my tornado of a week, but as from tomorrow morning, I was going to concentrate hard and see if I could find Mushu a new, loving, responsible home (i.e. nowhere near Kyra).

Then I was going to start a brand new journal, since my old one was long gone. And the first thing I was going to write in it? A joke.

Q. What's the difference between Feargal O'Leary and a seat with drawing pins glued to it?

A. None – they're *both* a complete pain in the bum...

Chapter 18

TWINKLE, TWINKLE, LITTLE BULB...

Fairgrounds are like fairyland at night, aren't they? When the sun goes down and all those endless garlands and garlands of coloured bulbs start sparkling. It's enough to make you forget your troubles and get you feeling all sparkly yourself...

"Ally Love, you look *gorgeous*," Billy crooned at me.

I did *not* look gorgeous. I looked like a walrus crossed with a knock-kneed stork. On crutches.

"Thank you, darling," I crooned back at his full-length reflection in the mirror. "You look pretty darn gorgeous yourself."

"Yeah, I know," Billy grinned. "Specially when I do *this*!"

Billy went up on his toes, instantly expanding his head to hot-air balloon proportions. With his unfeasibly short legs, he was a dead ringer for a mutant Mr Potato-Head.

Round the corner in the Hall of Mirrors we

heard the unmistakable cackle of Kyra, joined by all the other girls cracking up.

"What?" I grinned, hobbling my way round to see what was so funny, followed closely by Mr Mutant Potato-Head.

Poor Sandie, at least she's a good sport. Even though everyone was in fits, she stood still, all the better for us all to get a gawp at the version of her that consisted of a Barbie-sized body attached to a ship's bow-sized nose. (And a red one at that.)

"Hey!" Billy yelped above the girly squealing going on. "Who's for the bumper cars next?"

"Not me," I mumbled.

"Why not, spoilsport?" Billy demanded.

"Because I don't need whiplash as well as torn ligaments," I pointed out. "*And* there's nowhere to put your crutches in a bumper car."

"Ally…" said Billy dreamily, coming right up close to my face. "Tonight is special. Tonight, all your dreams will come true. Tonight, Ally, I will take care of every single one of your wishes, desires and worries."

Please, Mr Joker. *Give* me a break.

"Billy," I smiled broadly at him, "tonight, I will happily poke my crutch in your eye if you try and force me on to *any* fairground ride I don't want to go on."

I thought I was making my point.

I didn't realize (although I *should* have) that saying no to Billy when he was in *that* kind of a silly mood was a really, *really* big waste of time.

"All right?"

"No," I replied, crossing my arms and staring off over the bumper-car rink at my friends, who included Sandie – holding on tightly to the crutches I'd given her when Billy had forced me to hop-hop my way over to this particular red car with him.

And it hadn't started with the bumper car.

Oh, no.

As soon as we'd all wriggled our way out of the wibbly-weird Hall of Mirrors, Chloe had demanded a go on the Ghost Train (Jen held my crutches for that, as Sandie and I screamed our way through a surprisingly unscary ride of flashing lights and crêpe-paper streamers tickling our necks), and then Kellie had squealed and squealed until we'd all gone on the old-fashioned "Chair-o-Plane" ride. Actually, the grumpy forty-something-year-old guy running the "Chair-o-Plane" didn't look *too* chuffed at having to store my crutches in his cabin-thing with him. You know, the only thing that made him shrug OK at the very idea of stashing my metal alien pets (as Winslet might have described them, if she could talk rather than growl), was that he might lose out on eight fares if me, Sandie, Kyra, Chloe, Kellie, Jen, Salma and Billy had chosen to hobble off in a different direction.

Kellie held my crutches when me and Kyra strapped ourselves into the Octopus ride. That was one I *really* wish I hadn't gone on; not 'cause of my dodgy ankle, but because during the five minutes it took to fill up all the empty spaces on board, Kyra had managed to totally embarrass me at the top of her voice. It was all because – while dangling from our seats – I'd spotted and pointed out the rubbish actor and his family; the not-so-nice new neighbours I'd had the misfortune to meet at Michael and Harry's barbecue. Very stupidly, I went and giggled to Kyra about them – telling her about all the naff acting jobs Mr Actor had been boasting about. And what does Kyra go and do? She only yells out, "Oi, Mister! Were you in *The Bill?* Heard you were lousy! Ha, ha, ha, ha!"

Honestly, I didn't know where to look (there's nowhere much to hide when you're stuck two metres up in the air strapped into a metal chair). What was Kyra like? Like a hyperactive gremlin, tonight, for some reason.

So ... there had been the Ghost Train, the

circa 1950s "Chair-o-Plane" ride, the Octopus, a few assorted Blast-a-Frog/Shoot-a-Duck/Thump-a-Squirrel type sideshow games we'd tried (that Tor would have hyperventilated at, even if all the animals *were* made out of rubber), and then – finally – I was *made* to go on the dodgems.

"It'll be fun!" Billy grinned at me.

"If my ankle gets hurt, I'll hold you personally responsible!" I narrowed my eyes at him.

But he wasn't listening. Like every person behind every wheel of every dodgem car, Billy was grinning an inanely competitive grin. Whether it was that teeth-grinding, ten-year-old kid over there, or the grim-faced OAP with his slightly wary-looking granddaughter riding nervous pillion; everyone was gearing up to – and let's not mince our words here – *thunk* the heck out of every other bumper car on the rink. And it wasn't just the scarily determined ten-year-old, or the over-enthusiastic OAP – it was everyone else. It was that guy over there ... and that weird bloke over there. Everyone was waiting for the off; for the second that the music would start up and the electricity would flicker through the wires and down into the cabs.

"Ready?" Billy grinned at me, gripping the wheel.

"No!" I insisted stupidly, as the car lurched forward, electricity wired at full-on.

"To infinity ... and *beyond*!" Billy giggled, thumping straight into the first bumper car that happened to lurch into our path.

Bumper cars are called bumper cars for a reason. In the space of about five seconds, we'd *thunk*ed into five cars, all intent on barging into me and Billy, and all jiggling my wonky ankle around in ways that were in danger of causing extra, excruciating pain.

"What are those guys playing at? They keep coming straight for us!" I heard Billy shout, just before another bumper car crashed nose-first into us.

Billy took control, steering our car away from the thunking it had just had ... at the hands of two lads, one dopey white, one quite-cute black.

It was almost as if Mikey D and Feargal O'Leary had aimed directly at us...

"That thing was fixed..." mumbled Billy, as we walked over towards the hot-dog stand.

"Billy, it *wasn't* fixed – Sandie won a prize fair and square," I told him. "You're just a bad loser, and I think you should buy her a hot dog too, just to show her you didn't mean it."

Even in the fairy-lit darkness, I could see the small smile of victory on Sandie's face. (Peeking just above the fuzzy pink face of Winnie the Pooh's sidekick, Piglet.) I think she was probably as surprised as Billy that she'd beaten him on the Test-Your-Strength machine.

Me, Billy and Sandie had left Kyra and the others piling on the dodgems for another round of thunking. But after being thunked too much for a girl with a wonky ankle, all *I* wanted was to take it easy for a bit and eat the hot dog Billy had promised me. Then, on the way to the food van, his eyes had lit up at the sight of the Test-Your-Strength machine and he insisted he had to have a go (pity there wasn't a Spot-the-Braincell machine). So, *blam!* he brings the mallet down hard as he can, and *shoof!* the metal ball zaps up about a metre high (i.e. two metres short of the bell). "D'you fancy a go?" the guy running the machine grinned at Sandie – who knows why; probably because she looks like she's got muscles with all the strength of cooked spaghetti. But what *I* knew and the fairground guy *didn't*, was that my buddy Snotty may be shy, but she's *very* stubborn. After shaking her head at him a few times, Sandie seemed to realize she was being teased, and deter-mination took over. Grabbing the mallet, she took one deep breath, and *blam!* was quickly followed by *ping!*

"He could have done something round the back – pulled some lever or something that made it easier," Billy grumbled on.

"Billy, are you *that* desperate for a Piglet?" I quizzed him. " 'Cause if you're that upset, I'll go and buy you one, since you didn't win it!"

"Here," giggled Sandie, thrusting Piglet at Billy. "You can have a cuddle, if you want!"

"Ha, ha, ha…" Billy mumbled, pushing the soft toy away.

But he was laughing, you could tell. Even if he knew he was going to have to cough up for two hot dogs after this. Hope he'd brought enough money with—

Oh.

I'd been fooling around with Billy and Sandie and Piglet too much to notice that we'd arrived at the hot-dog stand. I wasn't particularly surprised to see Kyra and Chloe and everyone there – after all, it's where we said we'd meet up with them. I was more surprised to see that they were all chatting and laughing … with Feargal O'Leary and his meat-head mates.

"Hey, guess what?" Chloe grinned excitedly, as soon as she spotted us. "Kyra's having a party! Right now – back at her place!"

Everyone was smiling at the news. Everyone,

including Mikey D, Mikey F, Ishmail, Baz and Feargal O'Leary.

Maybe I was totally wrong (as if), but it looked suspiciously like they'd got themselves an invite to the party too.

What did Billy say earlier about all my dreams coming true tonight? More like my nightmares...

Chapter 19

AM I HAVING FUN YET?

"Kyra!" Kellie called out, over the top of the blaring music.

Kyra didn't seem to hear – she was too busy trying to drag a reluctant (but grinning) Feargal O'Leary up to dance with her and Chloe and Jen.

Meanwhile, Sandie and Salma had – for no apparent reason – swapped shoes, and Salma was making Sandie sashay, model-style, up and down beside the French doors in ridiculously high strappy sandals, while Mikey D and Ishmail whooped encouragingly. Sandie ought to be careful – the way she was wobbling, I'd have to lend her my crutches by the end of the night.

"What's up with your face?" frowned Billy, flopping down beside me and sploshing splashes of Coke out of the two glasses he'd brought over.

"Nothing," I frowned back, automatically patting my face for signs of it swelling, or bits of it falling off or whatever it was that was making Billy stare at me that way.

"It's just that it's … it's…" Billy wrinkled up his nose as he examined my face up close. "It's *miserable*. That's what it is."

Oh, that.

Well, maybe my miserable expression was down to the fact that right before the dancing started, the entertainment for the party seemed to consist of laughing at *me*.

First, Kyra had started joking about body-searching Feargal for my missing journal, and then Chloe had started fooling around and asking what I'd got written down in there anyway – was it lists of boys I fancied or what? I was *way* too mortified to do anything more than sit silently, sending out psychic bad vibes in the direction of Chloe and Kyra.

And then this conversation began about nick-names and my heart just sank, dreading one of the lads bringing up the "Blue Bum" thing. I was still holding my breath when I heard Salma get cheeky with Feargal and ask him how come he hadn't tried to give himself a great nickname, seeing as his real name suited him about as much as if the Queen was called "Bob". But before Feargal could reply, Sandie went all giggly and told everyone the stupid story about how we'd given each other nicknames at the school party the night before.

I mean, the Marquise of Snotsville and Lady Hopalong of Hornsey ... they weren't *meant* to be cool. It was just some dumb thing we came up with out of sheer, total boredom. Nobody else was meant to hear about them. You should have heard the way everyone started cracking up at that, like they were the most cringingly pathetic nicknames they'd ever heard.

And the worst thing was, they were *right*...

"*Kyra!*" Kellie yelped louder from the living-room doorway.

"Wonder what she wants?" I muttered aloud.

"Oh, it's probably something to do with the exploding beans..." Billy shrugged beside me.

"*What* exploding beans?!" I turned and quizzed him, mystified.

"The ones Baz and Mikey F just blew up in the kitchen while I was getting us these drinks," Billy replied matter-of-factly.

"Billy, *why* were they blowing up beans?"

"Huh?" he muttered, his attention suddenly drawn to Ishmail, who was at that very minute sniggering and wobbling his way along the carpet wearing his gang's trademark baggy jeans, hooded sweatshirt, chunky jacket – and Salma's very high sandals.

Honestly, how could Billy come out with a statement like that and assume it's explanation enough?

"I said *why* were Baz and Mikey F blowing up beans in the kitchen?"

"Uh, I don't think they *meant* to," Billy shrugged. "They were trying to make beans on toast for everyone and they put the beans in the microwave. But I think they used the wrong type of container or something, 'cause the beans kind of exploded inside. And then they splatted some more when Baz tried to take them out. There's orange bean stuff all over the place."

I hadn't the faintest clue what Baz and Mikey F could have done to make the mighty bean explosion happen. Maybe if I didn't have my crutches and maybe if Kyra wasn't being so annoying tonight (she was *so* showing-off in front of Feargal and Co), I might have gone through and tried to help clear up the mess before Mr and Mrs Davies got home after their night out. But I didn't.

Specially not after Kyra had showed me up in front of the actor bloke earlier at the fair. OK, so I didn't like him very much, but he was still my neighbour; *Kyra* didn't have to risk bumping into him when she was buying her *Just 17* at the local newsagents, did she? And another thing – why had she got so instantly buddy-buddy with Feargal, when she knew I didn't like the guy?

"*KYRA!*" Kellie yelled again, going over and turning the music down.

"What?" grumbled Kyra, grinding to a reluctant halt. She and Chloe and Jen had been clasping hands, spinning around a trapped Feargal who was stuck in the middle of all three of them.

"The kitchen's a total state!" Kellie blurted out. "Baz and Mikey blew up something in the micro-wave!"

"Sorry, Kyra…" muttered a soulful, bean-covered Baz from the living-room doorway.

Mikey F was standing behind him, orange sauce splattered on his pale face like freckles.

For a second, Kyra narrowed her eyes, then started giggling.

"I've *got* to see this!" she sniggered, letting go of Chloe and Jen's hands and freeing Feargal at the same time.

"My mum would *kill* me if that happened in our house," Billy observed, as Kyra bounded, laughing and carefree, through into the hallway that led to the kitchen.

"Kyra's mum is going to kill her for that happening, too," I told him. "Specially since they've been fighting all week over the cat and everything."

"Yeah…" Billy nodded thoughtfully. "When you

were in the loo earlier she asked me if I fancied taking Mushu off her hands."

"What?"

"Uh-huh," Billy nodded gravely. "She offered to buy me any Gameboy game I wanted if I took the kitten off her."

God, what was Kyra like? You know, up on Crouch End Broadway at weekends, there's a whole bunch of stalls set up, selling second-hand books and crafts and stuff. If it wasn't for the fact that she'd dumped Mushu on my family, I wouldn't put it past Kyra to set up her own *kitten* stall right beside them all.

Kyra was unbelievable. What was she going to surprise me with next?

I didn't have long to wait before I found out.

"Hey!" a gleeful Kyra called out, as she bounded back into the room clutching what looked like an empty bottle of mineral water or something. "Look what I found! Guess what we can use this for?"

Um ... putting in the recycling bin? Wow, this party was getting less fun by the second.

"Right, *first* spin is to see who goes first – OK?" Kyra beamed at us all.

We were sitting in a circle on the living-room

floor, with the empty bottle resting on its side on the carpet in the centre of the circle.

"Go on, then!" Chloe urged Kyra, dying to get the game started.

Me ... I felt my ankle throb and my stomach lurch. Part of me wished I'd gone home before this stupid game ever started, or even right after the fair. And then again ... some ridiculous part of me felt almost excited about this dumb game of Spin the Bottle. How crazy is that?

"And it's..." Kyra gave the bottle a twirl. "...Kellie! You're first to go, Kel!"

Even with her dark skin, you could tell Kellie was blushing. (At least her skin only goes marginally darker and glowy, whereas *I* turn into a big red radish-head whenever *I* blush.)

Everyone was clapping and cheering – even me, though I don't really understand why – when Kellie nervously did her spin.

"*Bazzzzzz!!*" yelled eleven over-excited voices, as Kellie and Baz went into spasms of shyness.

For a second, neither of them moved, too embarrassed to say or do anything, then Baz scrambled across the circle on his hands and knees, landed a smacker on Kellie's cheek, then scrambled back just as quickly to his spot while everyone cheered and clapped, apart from Kyra, who booed loudly.

"You *cheats*! It's supposed to be on the *lips*!" Kyra giggled, as Baz took his turn and the bottle twirled round to point at ... Kyra.

"Oh, yeah?" Baz grinned. "Come on then!"

The whooping was deafening, as Kyra leant towards Baz and gave him a quick, full-on smooch on the lips.

And after that, the bottle spun on ... with Kyra kissing Ishmail, then Ishmail kissing Chloe, then Chloe's spin pointing to Jen, which was quickly re-spun to point at Mikey D, who kissed her before taking his own turn and kissing Salma, who then got Billy – weird! – and then Billy (blushing furiously) spun and got ... Sandie! (*Very* weird, considering their history of not getting on at all well.) Cue the quickest of tight-lipped kisses, and Sandie spun on to Mikey D (yells of "Not again! Not fair!", while Mikey D smirked happily), who then kissed Jen, whose turn spun her round to Feargal, who then took his turn and the bottle twirled round and round and round in slow motion, ending up slowing ... slowing ... *slowwwiiinnggggg* up directly in front of...

Who else?

Me.

I'd been getting used to his weird stares over the course of the week, but I suddenly couldn't stand him staring at me with his big, chocolatey-brown eyes right now. The thought of us leaning across towards each other, of him wrapping an arm around behind me, of those eyes gazing into mine, as his lips drew closer to mine ... the warmth of them ... the very closeness of—

"I can't do this!" I whispered urgently, scrambling around for my crutches and hoisting myself – with minimal grace – to my feet.

"Ally!"

"What's up?"

"Aww, come on!"

"Al!"

"What's going on?"

"Al, what's wrong?"

I could hear them all calling, but I was already gone, thudding my way out into the hall, struggling to get my cardie off the hook of the coat-rack.

Then I heard footsteps following me out – Sandie's of course; my faithful friend, coming to my rescue, ready to stand by me and be by my side as I (slowly) hobbled home...

"Ally? Don't go..."

The voice was soft and low. And *male*, if I wasn't very much mistaken. Only I couldn't turn round as I was temporarily in a knot of cardigan, arms and crutches.

I felt someone grab hold of one crutch and help me out of my tangle at the same time as I felt my face flush furiously.

"I'm fine!" I muttered impatiently, as I wriggled an arm into the sleeve of my cardie and felt tears of embarrassment prickle in my eyes. I couldn't even *look* at Feargal.

"Sit down ... just for a second. *Please*, Ally."

His face I wasn't focussing on, but – my head held low – I saw his hand gesture to the staircase.

Right at that second, I didn't have the energy (or the ability) to flounce out of Kyra's front door, so I sat; plopping myself bum-first on to the carpet-covered steps, clattering my crutches together, and staring resolutely at the floor.

What did he want, that Feargal O'Leary? To humiliate me some more? Was he planning on telling me I was a total chicken for running out on some stupid game? Or was he going to read out more mortifying excerpts of the journal he'd nicked from me?

Without looking up, I could feel him settle down beside me on the step, and waited for the humiliation to follow. And waited, and waited... All I could hear (apart from the blood pounding through my head) was the music being turned up again in the living room.

"What?" I said finally, when I couldn't stand the silence between me and Feargal any more.

"I…"

I held my breath, waiting for the punchline, but it didn't come.

"What?" I demanded, fear suddenly making me braver, as I finally lifted my head to stare at him.

His face was hard to read. With his hood down, up close, there was no trace of the hard-man glare. He looked … pretty. Gorgeous dark brown skin, high cheekbones, full, soft lips, eyes full of words that he wasn't saying…

Oh, who was *I* kidding. Feargal O'Leary was about to rip me to shreds. He'd read my journal and was ready to tear into me by quoting back all the romantic lyrics and silly thoughts and fancy bits of poetry I'd scribbled down in there. When he said them out loud back to me, they'd sound hollow and silly … not inspirational like I'd meant them to be.

I dropped my head in my hands and waited for him to start. What was it going to be? The lyrics from "Not Enough…" again? Or maybe that bit out of that brilliant poem by—

"Ally … I really like you."

Um…

"I mean, I think you're really ... brilliant and amazing and stuff."

Stuff. I was brilliant and amazing and stuff.

Wow.

My mum used to whisper to me that I was her little pumpkin. I was Dad's darling Ally Pally. Grandma loved me loads, just as much as she loved Linn and Rowan and Tor. And Tor and Rowan and Linn loved me, even if they only showed it by doing stuff like letting me have the last handful of popcorn in the bowl or whatever. And Rolf and Winslet and Colin and Co let me know they loved me by licking me with their pet-food-scented tongues, or by choosing my bed (out of many others) to curl up on in the middle of the night. Sandie and Billy and my other friends let me know that they liked me, just because they ... er ... hung out with me.

But nobody, *nobody* had ever told me I was brilliant and amazing and stuff.

"Eeemphhh."

It was all that came out of my mouth in response to what Feargal had just said.

"Here..."

The "here" referred to the thing he was passing me. My journal.

"Oh..." I said quietly, feeling the familiar, mock-suede fabric between my fingers. I still couldn't look at Feargal.

"I'm sorry I nicked it from your pocket," I heard him mumble. "I did it 'cause I wanted to see what was in there. And it's really funny and brilliant and everything."

OK.

I wasn't just brilliant and amazing and stuff ... but my journal was funny and brilliant and everything.

Wow...

"Um, thank you," I mumbled, stroking my hand over the cover of my long-missing notebook, and referring to all Feargal's compliments at once. I hope he understood.

"Ally," I heard him sigh softly, "I really—"

I really don't know what he "really" ... whatever. From our vantage point – at the bottom of the stairs facing the front door – Feargal and I were in prime position to observe Kyra's parents return early from their night out and stumble into an unexpectedly crowded, noisy, bean-splattered house.

Her mum and dad frowned wordlessly at me and Feargal. Or maybe they just didn't bother to try and talk because the music was blaring so loud that they'd never have been heard.

"Kyra! What on earth is going on here?" we just

about heard Mrs Davies yell, as Feargal helped me to my feet and we followed her and Mr Davies down the hall.

Mrs Davies stopped in the living-room doorway as Mr Davies continued down the hall. Over Mrs Davies's shoulder, I could just make out Kyra leaping away from Mikey F, who the bottle must have pointed at.

"Oh my God!!" I heard Mr Davies call out loudly from the kitchen.

Uh-oh ... he must have spotted the bean explosion. Maybe it was time for all of us to get out of here *fast*.

Or fast*ish*, in *my* hopalong case...

Chapter 20

GRANDMA'S SNOOZLY SURPRISE...

Ah! The first day of the holidays and freedom! And the first words I'm woken with are: "Can we get some hamster chews?"

It was only half-past eight and Tor was already dressed and ready to do our regular Saturday morning pet-shop expedition.

Yep, life in the Love household was carrying on as usual – holidays or not – but I wasn't sure if the same could be said for the Davies household.

I couldn't help wondering (and worrying about) what was going on with Kyra... Last night, her mum and dad had started flipping out at her in front of us all, telling her off for having a party without asking, and worse still, yelling at her for redecorating their designer kitchen with tomato sauce and bean splodges. At that point, Kyra had stormed stoney-faced out of the room, and we all heard her stomping upstairs and slamming a door shut. I didn't feel too brave in the face of such parental anger, but I ended up stammering something about us all being sorry, then Chloe started to explain that the bean explosion was an accident, but I don't think Mr and Mrs Davies were in the mood to listen – they asked us to please go, and there wasn't much more we could do than just that.

When we got outside, all of us were so stunned that everyone just drifted off in little groups towards wherever was home, leaving me, Sandie and Billy hobbling towards Billy's bus stop before us girls carried on along the road. Feargal... Well, Feargal and his mates lived in the opposite direction.

Hmm. What a weird end to a truly weird week...

I managed to convince Tor that we were way too early for the pet shop, and plonked him in front of the TV for an hour, while I wriggled my way carefully in and out of the shower (very tricky when you're trying to hold a bandaged leg away from any water), and tried to wake myself up some more with breakfast.

"Can we go now?" asked Tor, magically appearing by my side in his jacket as soon as I finished my last mouthful of toast.

"Uh, OK," I shrugged, knowing that resistance was futile. Tor was doing what Rolf and Winslet did when they were waiting for their walk –

following me around like a hairy shadow and fixing their big, guilt-trip eyes on me.

But just as I was hopping along the hallway in search of my shoe (fifty per cent of my footwear collection was redundant, thanks to my mummified leg), the phone rang.

"Hello?" I said, still slightly sleepily.

"Ally? It's me," yawned a voice from the other end of the line.

"Oh, hi, Kyra," I replied, recognizing that yawn straight away.

(Tor, standing right by my side, doggy-style, let out a big sigh now he realized the pet-shop expedition was going to be put on pause for a few minutes.)

"Mad night, last night, wasn't it?" said Kyra, stating the obvious.

"What happened after we left?" I frowned down the phone.

Funny ... she didn't sound as freaked out as I'd thought she would this morning.

"Er, shouting, shouting and some more shouting, I guess," Kyra replied flippantly.

"Yeah, but what actually *happened*?" I asked, trying to get her to be more informative.

"Well, once Mum and Dad stopped yelling, I took another look at the kitchen and started to feel pretty bad, so I said sorry about the mess. And sorry for having people round the house without asking first. And then ... then it all got a bit strange."

Her voice had changed from typical Kyra cocky to something far more wobbly.

"Strange how?"

"Strange like Mum getting a bit tearful," Kyra said in a quieter voice, as if she didn't want anyone overhearing. (She should try that same voice in class sometime – it could stop her getting detention so often.)

"What was she upset about?"

"Um ... she said she hated us fighting all the time. She said she wanted us to be friends, like we used to be when I was little," Kyra sighed.

"Wow. What did you say then?" I asked.

"I said sorry for fighting too, and that it would be nice to be friends..." Kyra mumbled, sounding pleased and embarrassed all at the same time.

That was really nice if they'd reached a bit of a truce. Specially since Kyra had the luxury of being in the same room as her mum whenever she wanted, which was more than *I* had...

"That's great," I mumbled, glad for Kyra and suddenly slightly sad for me.

"Yeah, but *then*," Kyra continued, sounding

more like her bouncy self all of a sudden, "Mum announced that I could keep Mushu, if I wanted!"

Urgh... I didn't know whether to be pleased or worried about that news. After her first attempts at caring for Mushu, Kyra hadn't exactly come across as a likely candidate for any Pet-Owner of the Year awards. But maybe it would be OK, if her parents were involved now too. Maybe—

"But I just said 'nah'," Kyra carried on breezily. "It's too much hassle looking after kittens, with all that litter-tray business and feeding them and everything!"

Instantly, all my sympathy for Kyra took wings and fluttered off out the window.

What *was* she like?

"And what about Mushu?" I asked, fuming quietly.

"Don't worry!" Kyra yawned. "I'll sort something out."

Yeah – she'd sort something out. Sometime, *never*.

"So, hey!" I heard Kyra giggle. "What went on with you and Feargal last night?"

"Oh, sorry, Kyra – can't speak now, there's someone at the door..." I found myself launching into a lie. "Speak to you later – bye."

Tor's eyebrows furrowed together as he looked

at me, at the silent front door and back again.

I opened my mouth to explain about annoying friends and embarrassing situations and how you sometimes just don't want to talk about them and how little white lies can be quite handy sometimes – then I decided not to. Tor had plenty of time to find out about stuff like that himself when he got older.

"Right, pet shop! Let's go!" I beamed at him, nudging him out of the house with my crutch, before he could ask any awkward questions...

I'd been kind of preoccupied as me and Tor walked (and hobbled) along the road. In fact, I was so preoccupied that I hadn't taken much notice of the fact that Tor had insisted we go round past Grandma's flat before we headed up to the Broadway.

And I hadn't thought anything about the cardboard box he was carrying until it mewed.

"This is *such* a bad idea, Tor!" I told him, as we let ourselves into Grandma's empty flat with the spare key she always left with us.

"No it's not!" said Tor brightly. "Come on, hurry! She'll be back soon!"

Tor Love ... he's a quiet kid, but you never know what strange plans and thoughts go on in that space-cadet mind of his. And this latest plan sounded like a truly lousy idea to me.

"All right, Mushu?" he whispered, placing the floppy, purring kitten on a cushion on Grandma's favourite chair.

Mushu blinked lazily, gazed around the immaculately tidy room with his tiny button eyes, and curled up to sleep quite happily.

"Did you tell Dad you were going to do this, Tor?" I asked warily.

"Not exactly," he said, shrugging a seven-year-old shrug at me.

Here's what had happened: it turns out that it wasn't just me who was worried about the effect Mushu was having on Tor and the neglected Love zoo. While I'd been out at the fair and at Kyra's the night before, Dad had had a little bedtime chat with my brother, talking about how it wasn't fair to the other animals that Mushu was getting so much attention. He told Tor that Mushu really needed a home all to himself, where he could be spoiled and loved, without putting any other animals' (wet) noses out of joint.

(I guess Dad was also pointing out in a roundabout way that maybe we couldn't afford yet another furry mouth to feed, since we already had about a million.)

So Tor had slept on the problem, and come up with his lousy plan – sneaking Mushu into Grandma's flat and affections while he knew she would be out at her Over-50s exercise class.

"But Tor, do you think Grandma actually *wants* a pet?" I asked, thinking that what I really meant was, "But Tor, doesn't Grandma actually *hate* animals?"

"She likes Mushu. She said he's not as hairy as the others," Tor stated.

Hmm ... well that was praise indeed, coming from Grandma.

"And Mushu will stop her being lonely," muttered Tor, adjusting the hand-written label he'd tied on to Mushu's collar with ribbon.

I tilted my head to read what it said: *Can I come and live with you, please?*

"Come on!" said Tor, tugging at my arm. "We've got to go! She'll be back any minute!"

"Oh, I don't know about this..." I muttered, staring down at the dozy bundle of fur. "What if Grandma goes off out somewhere after her exercise class and doesn't come back for hours?"

Tor sighed a big, fed-up sigh and looked wearily at me.

"Too late now..." he said, a second before Grandma's keys rattled in the lock.

(Like Billy always says, Tor is a bit of a Spook-kid. Either that or he's got the hearing of a bat with a pair of radars for ears.)

"What's going on here?" asked Grandma, looking confused.

Tor only grinned broadly in response, while I stayed stupidly silent, frozen like a statue at being caught out.

Grandma walked over to the chair, peered over her glasses at the sleeping form of Mushu, who very conveniently chose that very moment to open his brown button eyes and purr appealingly.

"What does this say?" Grandma asked us, as she held up the label to read.

Mushu nuzzled her fingers and purred so much he got the hiccups. He couldn't be more cute if he tried.

"Just keep him for the weekend and see if you like him, Grandma!" Tor beamed.

"You can take him back to ours, if it doesn't work out – promise!" I quickly assured her.

Grandma tutted loudly and narrowed her eyes at me and Tor in turn, but I noticed that her index finger was brushing around Mushu's ear.

"Me and Ally have to go to the pet shop now!" Tor said hurriedly, shoving me and my crutches towards the front door before Grandma got a chance to get a word in edgeways. "Bye!"

You know, it's amazing how fast you can hop down a flight of stairs and along the road when you don't want to get caught by a potentially irate gran...

Chapter 21

DOG-FOOD KISSES AND NOT-QUITE-DATES...

It's Sunday afternoon, and Grandma still hasn't come round to return the kitten, which me and Tor have taken to be a good sign.

Another good sign is that since Mushu got himself a loving new home (fingers crossed), it's been business as usual for the regular, motley Love pets. There are dog-eared, tail-less, moth-eaten cats draped purrily over every surface in the house, and scruffbag Rolf has turned into Tigger, bouncing around and slobbering licky kisses on everything that moves (which hasn't gone down well with some of the cats, who assume they're about to be eaten, I think). Grumpy old Winslet's great too – she hasn't growled once all day, even when we went to meet Billy, and his dumb dog Precious tried to sniff her bottom.

I, however, felt quite like growling when we met up with Billy. He's just a typical boy and *loves* it when he's right...

"Told you he fancied you!" Billy grinned at me,

as soon as I'd sat down next to him on the park bench.

"Shut up," I mumbled, hoping that he would.

Fat chance.

"*You* said he didn't, but *I* was right!"

"Billy..." I muttered darkly. "It was really hard work hobbling here to meet you with two dogs. Don't make me wish I'd stayed at home!"

(I'd managed with only one crutch today, which made it easier to hold on to leads and seemed to stress Winslet out less – though she still gave the evil alien pet a wide berth and a wary glance as we trundled to the park.)

"Wasn't I right, though? Say I was right about Feargal fancying you – go on, Ally!"

"I don't want to talk about it!"

"Ha! But I was right, and you just don't want to admit it!"

OK, so he was right about being right, and right about me not wanting to admit it. Well, it's all too embarrassing, isn't it?

"Billy, shut up, or else..."

"Shut up or else what?"

"Or else..." I had to think fast. "Or else ... I *was* going to pay for us both to go out on the boating lake this morning, but maybe I won't bother now."

He's easy to bribe, my Billy (bless him). Five

minutes later we were on the other side of Alexandra Palace, sitting in a yellow plastic pedalo with three dogs wedged in the back, barking at passing ducks, while Billy was busy knocking himself out by pedalling for two. (Well, I couldn't help out, not with my dodgy ankle, could I?) And best of all, he didn't mention You-Know-Who once.

Result!

Speaking of You-Know-Who, I'd better go ... I'm meeting him in Priory Park in twenty minutes. Don't get *too* excited: it's not a date or anything.

"Do you want to, um, go for a walk or something tomorrow?" he'd asked, when he'd phoned me yesterday. (He'd gone round to Kyra's and got my number off her.)

"A walk?" I'd repeated stupidly, because the very fact that Feargal O'Leary had phoned up and asked me out had made my brain melt. I mean, I didn't know if I liked him, or *didn't* like him, or fancied him or *didn't* fancy him... And I *still* don't.

"Yeah, a walk," he laughed. "OK, so in your case, a hop!"

"Fine – I'll come," I replied, a little breathlessly. "On one condition..."

"What?"

"Don't make hopping jokes. And don't call me Hopalong. Or Blue Bum."

"Ally ... that's *three* conditions."

Urgh, I never was very good with maths.

"So?" I asked him, as Rolf started licking the toes of my mummified leg. "Is it a deal?"

"It's a deal."

And so, I have a deal ... and a not-quite-date, with a boy who was supposed to be tough but isn't really.

Hope he wears his hood down or he'll never hear a word I'm saying...

Wish me luck (gulp),

Ally :c)

PS Last night, I was flicking through my journal, and on the last page, there was joke scrawled in handwriting that definitely wasn't mine. It read, Q: *What's got four legs, a blue bum and a cute smile?*
A: *Ally Love (on crutches).*

PPS Might go and practise my "cute smile" in the mirror before I head out to meet Feargal. Just in case I feel like using it.
PPPS Is it normal to feel sick before a not-quite-date???

Coming soon:

Tattoos, Telltales and Terrible, Terrible Twins

"This place looks nuts!"

I'm pretty sure Sandie meant that in a good way. She's a huge fan of my family and our foibles (weird word, but then it's a weird family).

"Wow!" she exclaimed, flopping down on the deckchair beside the sofa and gazing up at the huge stained-glass-style sun that was taking up most of the living-room window.

"Nice, isn't it?" I grinned, pointing towards the sun (the fake one, not the real one, although that was out there somewhere beyond the window-pane). "Rowan made it out of these sheets of coloured plastic."

The daylight pouring through the yellow plastic turned the room even *more* yellow than it already was, giving it a totally tropical feel. "Looks jaundiced," Grandma mumbled when she checked it out ten minutes ago, just before Sandie turned up.

"Wish I could do stuff like this in *my* house,"

Sandie sighed, kicking her shoes off and making herself right at home. "Mum and Dad would flip out if I tried to stick up something like that in our front room!"

True. Mr and Mrs Walker have the dullest, most traditional house in the universe – apart from Sandie's room, of course, with those giant, mutant pink daisies that she and I painted on the walls one Sunday when her parents were out. They nearly had her adopted once they set eyes on that.

Maybe that's why Sandie's mum and dad were quite happy for her to come and stay with me for a week, while they got their place totally done up before the baby was born. Perhaps they were worried that she'd end up persuading the decorators to do subversive stuff like hang the wallpaper upside down or fit portholes in all the doors or something.

Whatever, a couple of minutes ago she dumped one super-huge holdall outside in our hallway – which helped with the house's overall holiday theme, I guess.

"Ally! And Sandie!" I heard Dad call through from the kitchen. "Tea's nearly ready. Do you girls want to come through? I just want to have a bit of a chat with everyone!"

"Ooh, it must be about your visitors! How exciting!"

"Yeah..." I replied dubiously, stepping over the donkey ring and a conked-out Rolf, who was doing an impression of a semi-live bearskin rug.

To be honest, I wasn't sure what I thought about these visitors. I'd tried to scrutinize Dad's face for clues when he told us about the phone call from his long-lost brother he'd just taken back at the shop, but it seemed to register more blank shock than bolt-out-of-the-blue pleasant surprise, which wasn't too promising.

"What're your uncle and aunt like?" asked Sandie, following me through to the kitchen.

"Can't remember," I told her truthfully.

I was four when my uncle Joe and his wife emigrated to Canada. I have a *few* memories from around that age – like being sick on my dad when he played aeroplanes with me over his head, and watching six-year-old Rowan go hysterical after idly ramming Barbie's sandal up her nostril and jamming it there – but I've got no memories at all of Uncle Joe and Auntie Pauline. "We never saw that much of them," I remember Mum once telling me. "Your dad and his brother are like chalk and cheese. There wasn't a problem; they just didn't have much in common, and drifted apart over the years."

They drifted apart all right. Oceans apart, once

Uncle Joe jaunted off to Canada. Apparently, Dad had tried writing loads of times (phoning was a bit too expensive), but Uncle Joe never got round to replying, and Dad's letters petered out in the vacuum. For most of the time, it's been a case of exchanging a lone Christmas card once a year. In his, Dad's always written a little note to say how we're all doing. In Uncle Joe's, all there is is a "Happy Doodah" type message – the same one they send to everyone – plus an up to date photo of his kids: nine-year-old twins called (wait for it) Carli and Charlie. Actually, there's always a scuffle between me, Linn, Ro and Tor when Uncle Joe's card arrives, simply because – if you want to know the ugly truth – we're all dying to see how much weirder-looking our Canadian cousins have got one year on. I mean, take babies: they're usually round and blobby and cute, right? Not our cousins. Just months old, they looked more like bad-tempered elves than anything else. And time hasn't done them any favours; they get just a little bit bigger, a little bit elfier with every passing year…

That's so rotten of me to say, I know. Maybe they stood staring unsmiling at the camera because they hated getting their picture taken. Maybe they were really nice and friendly (and not so elfy) when you got to meet them in the flesh.

Well, I'd be finding out pretty soon. In about eighteen hours, to be exact.

"Still, I think it's *very* odd to travel halfway around the world without giving you a bit more notice that he was coming!" Grandma was saying to Dad, as he settled down on a chair at the kitchen table.

Despite it being Rowan's turn to make tea (she was just serving up an amazingly edible mix of salad-type stuff, plus – eek! – a bowl of cold Spaghetti Hoops), the table – laid out with paper plates, plastic cutlery and glasses complete with jaunty cocktail umbrellas – was a pretty popular place to be this evening. Dad was plonked at one end, surrounded by Linn, Rowan, Grandma and Stanley, who was becoming something of a regular fixture round at ours. Which was fine – he's a really nice bloke, apart from clumps of white hair that stick out of his ears, but it's not like he can really help that. (Though shouldn't barbers do a nose and ear hair-trim service? They could do specials: "Free ear trim with every cut and blow dry!")

Apart from those five, there was a chair and an old stool set aside for me and Sandie. At first I couldn't see Tor – and then I caught a glimpse of the top of his head. He was sitting (just above floor level) on another of our saggy, stripy deckchairs, which he must have dragged in from the garden to solve the chair-shortage problem. Rolf (if he ever woke up) and Winslet were going to *love* that – he was a perfect height to feed them snacklets off his plate without Grandma's stern disapproval spoiling the fun.

"Irene –"

(It's always very strange to hear Grandma called anything other than "Grandma".)

"– once my brother gets something in his head, there's nothing much you can do to stop him," Dad explained, leaning forward and helping himself to the food. "He probably thought it'd be an excellent idea to turn up and surprise us – like something off a TV show!"

"But doesn't he think for a minute that it might not be a convenient time for you?" Grandma continued, frowning. "And I mean, it isn't, is it? You're off to that important bike fair next Wednesday, aren't you?"

Grandma (and her kitten Mushu) were going to be moving in with us from Wednesday to Saturday, to make sure we all ate properly and that Rolf and Winslet didn't have any wild parties for all the neighbourhood dogs while Dad was away.

"Well, I think I'll have to ditch that plan now," Dad shrugged fatalistically. "I can't exactly go swanning off when this is the one chance I get to see Joe in years. And another thing; I kind of need your help over the next couple of weeks, guys…"

Dad gazed around the table, his eyes resting specifically on me, Rowan, Linn and Tor.

"Help how?" asked Linn.

"Well, I can't exactly afford to shut the shop for days on end while Joe and everyone are here, but what I thought I'd do is call Rory – he was going to cover for me while I was at the bike fair. If he's not too busy I'll see if he can swap things around and let me have a couple of days off this week and a couple of days off next week instead."

"You mean you want *us* to look after Uncle Joe and Auntie Pauline and our cousins for the rest of the holiday?" said Rowan, probably already planning an exciting timetable of craft-related activities for the twins.

"Not exactly; not *all* the time." Dad shook his head. "I'm sure Joe's family have things they want to do and places they want to visit. But on the days I *do* have to work, if you kids wouldn't mind helping entertain Carli and Charlie a little bit, that would be great. And if they're anything like their dad, they'll like a good laugh…"

"Hey, didn't Uncle Joe once put your details in a Lonely Hearts ad without you knowing?" Linn asked, taking the coloured-paper umbrella out of her glass so that she could drink her orange juice without poking her eye out.

Good grief, I'd forgotten about that story. Dad (aged sixteen) knew nothing about it till he got a sackful of mail from women desperate to share his "luxury bachelor penthouse" and help him polish his "top of the range red Porsche". Thanks to Joe's "hilarious" prank, loads of lonely and easily impressed thirty-something women thought they were writing to a self-made paper-clip tycoon, not a teenage boy who lived in a council house with his mum, his annoying big brother and a rickety second-hand bike as his only form of transport.

"Yes, he did," Dad nodded, with a roll of his eyes.

"And didn't he get expelled from school for locking the music teacher in the cupboard when she went in to find the maracas?" I butted in, dredging up another old story from my memory banks.

"Yep," said Dad. "And then he took off the tape of *Peer Gynt* she'd been playing to the class and put on the Sex Pistols' 'God Save the Queen' instead."

Dad was actually smiling as he recounted that particular misdeed, but I think that's because he's a bit of a fan of punk music himself. Or I guess some of Uncle Joe's practical jokes seem funnier in hindsight than they were at the time.

"When you and Melanie got married – didn't Joe stand up and recite a rude limerick at the reception?" Grandma asked.

"Yes, Irene – that was Joe," Dad admitted. "I'm sorry that the one time you met him he was on his worst behaviour."

"What was the limerick?" I found myself asking.

"Never you mind, Ally. I just hope he's grown out of that silly behaviour," said Grandma, disapprovingly. (Couldn't you just have guessed that "Practical Jokes" are firmly on Grandma's list of Things She Doesn't Approve Of? I think they come somewhere between "Eating With Your Mouth Open" and "G-Strings".)

"Well, maybe being a parent has made him more sensible," Dad suggested. "But I wouldn't bet on it. Remember, this is the guy who wore a revolving bow tie at his *own* wedding."

Apparently, the vicar had got very cross, telling Uncle Joe that he wasn't taking the ceremony seriously and that he wouldn't carry on till Uncle Joe had switched his tie off.

"This should be an interesting visit..." Linn frowned. "So where are they going to be staying?"

"Well, that's what I wanted to talk to you

all about." Dad looked edgy. One hand was absently ruffling his short dark hair into mussed-up spikes; a nervous tic of his that's always a dead giveaway.

"So?" Rowan prompted him.

"So, they're coming to stay here."

As Dad spoke, he fixed his eyes firmly on the table, instead of glancing around at us all.

"Here?!" Linn barked. "Here *where*? There's only just enough room for *us* in this place! Why can't they stay in a hotel like normal people?"

I knew what Linn was thinking – she was just as curious as the rest of us about meeting our remote relatives, but for her, our house was chaotic enough without trying to shoehorn another entire family in between us and the army of pets.

"They *were* booked into a hotel, but I thought *this* way, it'd give us more of a chance to get to know each other. And the only place they'd managed to get at this time of the year was one of those rip-off B&Bs round Victoria that charge a fortune for a room the size of our garden shed," Dad shrugged. "I couldn't let them stay there – so I told them to come and bunk up with us."

"Speaking of sheds – I hope they realize that's where they're going to be sleeping!" said Linn, sticking her thumb in the direction of the garden.

She loves Dad like mad, but I think she despairs of his ditziness sometimes.

"Like a holiday cabin!" came an enthusiastic voice from (nearly) under the table.

"No, Tor, we can't let them sleep out in the garden shed," Dad shook his head. "That's why I thought we should sit down and talk about how we can do this."

"Maybe we could clear out the attic cupboard – the twins could sleep in there. We could make it all cosy by chucking material over all the boxes and putting a little lamp, or some fairy lights in there!" said Rowan, her eyes gleaming at the opportunity of doing more inventive housey makeovers. "And Carli and Charlie should be small enough not to bump their heads on those low beams!"

"Small – like elves..." I heard Tor mutter to himself.

(I ducked my head under the table to see what he was up to, and spotted him cross-legged on the deckchair, spearing Spaghetti Hoops off his plate with the spiky end of his cocktail umbrella. Winslet was hunkered down on the floor beside him, ready to pounce on any stray hoops.)

"And where do you suggest Uncle Joe and Auntie Pauline sleep, Ro?" Linn flashed her eyes at our sister. "Standing up in the broom cupboard?!"

When you listen to some of her less-thought-out suggestions, it can seem like Rowan has the brain of a particularly tiny bird, and Linn is always keen to be the first one to point that out to her. But whatever, it *was* going to be a tight squeeze. How could three adults, three sisters, two cousins, a small brother and a Sandie all fit into our animal-infested zoo-cum-home?

"Nobody will be sleeping in any cupboards, or sheds, or tree houses, or whatever else," said Grandma firmly, accompanied by Stanley vehemently shaking his head in support. "There's got to be a sensible solution to this. And you children have to appreciate that your dad hasn't seen his brother for a long, long time, and I'm sure it's very important to him that you're all on your best behaviour when they arrive!"

I noticed Sandie twitching by my side, practically desperate to put her hand up and tell Grandma that she'd be good. I don't think she could believe her luck: up until a couple of days ago she thought she'd be hanging around her place watching paint dry, and now here she was in the midst of a proper family saga.

"Thanks, Irene," Dad said with a certain amount of relief in his voice. Grandma's a great referee, and even if she might not have thought much of our uncle on the one occasion she met him, she'd still give him the benefit of the doubt, and make sure we did the same.

"So, let's see," Grandma began, applying her ferociously logical brain to our housing problem. "For a start, the little boy can share with Tor, and— *Rowan!*"

At that very moment, Ro had leant across the table, catching Grandma's eye as she reached out for the enticing bowl of cold Spaghetti Hoops.

"Oh, sorry, Grandma," she began. "I just wanted some more of the—"

But the problem wasn't anything to do with rudeness or Spaghetti Hoops – it was to do with the heart-shaped garland of roses that was now peeking out from under the short sleeve of Rowan's pink T-shirt.

"Oh, *that*!" Ro exclaimed, as if it was the very first time she'd noticed the tattoo. "It's OK, Grandma – it's only a fake! It'll wash off in the shower!"

"It had better, young lady!" said Grandma, staring at my sister over the top of her gold-rimmed specs.

"Grandma, it's just a fashion thing. You *know* I'd never get a *real* tattoo!"

Tomorrow, we'd be seeing first-hand if there was any family resemblance between my dad and his prank-playing brother. But I'd just spotted a family resemblance between me and Ro that'd I'd never noticed before: a slight twitch at the side of her mouth. Could it be that she'd just told a porky-pie there?

Secret hair dyes and blatant lies … what exactly was Rowan up to?